FLY IN THE COBWEB

FLY IN THE COBWEB

FRANK PARRISH

1817

HARPER & ROW, PUBLISHERS, New York
Cambridge, Philadelphia, San Francisco, London
Mexico City, São Paulo, Singapore, Sydney

A DAN MALLETT NOVEL OF SUSPENSE

FIRST EDITION

Designer: Jénine Holmes

Library of Congress Cataloging-in-Publication Data

Parrish, Frank.
  Fly in the cobweb.

  "A Dan Mallett novel of suspense"—T.p. verso.
  I. Title.
PR6066.A713F6   1986   823'.914   85-45220
ISBN 0-06-015520-5

86 87 88 89 90 10 9 8 7 6 5 4 3 2 1

FLY IN THE COBWEB

1

THE PARISH OF MEDWELL FRATRORUM had two big houses. So small a community might have been expected to have only one house that looked as though it belonged to a squire, a lord of the manor, a knight of the shire. But Medwell had two. Had both been lived in as houses, rivalry—perhaps rancour—could have resulted, especially between the chatelaines. No doubt, eighty years ago, the lady of Medwell Priory and the lady of Medwell Court had vied in local display and in entertainment of resplendent house parties. But now there was no contest; only one of the two big houses was used as a private residence.

Medwell Priory had been a religious foundation of great antiquity, giving the village the Latin second half of its name. The prior and his brethren disappeared with the dissolution of the monasteries; the old stones of chapel and refectory were used to build pigsties; in the remaining ruins, for nearly four centuries, vagrants uncomfortably squatted. Then in 1905 a financier of complex ethnic origin caused a mansion to be built on the ancient site, of dark red brick, in the depressing taste of the time. Since it was uninhabitable, the great house was turned into a boarding school for little girls. The maids' bedrooms became dormitories; the park and paddocks became playing fields. It lay on the side of the parish in which Dan Mallett inconspicuously lived, in the crazy old cottage (once a gamekeeper's) about which his mother never stopped complaining; and the trees which dripped on the cottage formed the fringe of the Priory Woods. The woods were useful for rabbit holes, in which Dan kept money (current account), other money (deposit account, growing towards what was needful for his mother's hip operation), and various semi-precious objects (disposable assets, not acquired in the way of trade or inheritance). The woods were not otherwise of much use to Dan, being empty of game. The school was of no use at all.

Medwell Court was a different proposition, to Dan and to everybody else. It was large without being huge, grand without being pompous. Much of it was early Georgian. It had stables, coach house, staff cottages. It had been expensively and extensively modernised. Its preserves were crawling with pheasants;* on its small home farm prize cattle had been raised at staggering financial loss. It was a rich man's house. It was a highly desirable property which was, in some sort, jinxed. It was one of those places (of which everyone familiar with the English countryside knows examples) which keep changing hands. Its ancestral owners were bankrupted by the agricultural depression which followed the defeat of Napoleon; a succession of self-made men had come from the industrial north to set up as squires, and had either overreached themselves, grown bored or died without issue. Major March, in this tradition, had started strutting through the rooms of Medwell Court, in aggressive tweeds, in 1970, working hard at being the bluff and sporting countryman of whom he had read in novels; Major March, in his turn, was selling. It was said in the village that he was going

* The illicit midnight pursuit of which landed Dan Mallett in one of his most bizarre adventures; see *Snare in the Dark*, by the same author.

to Guernsey or the Bahamas or Bournemouth. Nobody much cared. His fourteen years' residence had not greatly impinged on the neighbourhood. He was just another rich outsider, here today and gone tomorrow. His successor would likely be the same sort of transient.

During Major March's regime, the Court was almost as useless to Dan Mallett as the Priory.

Most of the local nobs and near-nobs employed Dan for odd jobs and light gardening, less for what he did than for what he was. To them—transplanted townsfolk—he was essence of the English countryside, oak, ash and thorn in a tweed cap and ancient corduroys, fund of quaint proverbs and homespun wisdom, animated fossil from the remote rural past. He worked hard at all this, far harder than he worked in anybody's garden. From Thomas Hardy (writing about a Wessex already, in his time, long buried) he had acquired a dialect which the nobs could barely understand, but which enchanted them. In his rare moments of self-criticism he was aware of gross overacting: but it seemed to him that the more he hammed up his yokel-philosopher act the better the nobs liked it. The better they liked him. The more they trusted him. The easier, and more profitable, life became. It was something to do also with his small, spare figure, his unlined but deeply weatherbeaten face, his unruly mouse-coloured hair and his bright blue eyes. It was something to do with his smile. He had a number of smiles— they ranged from the little-boy-lecherous one he used on girls to the innocent-idiot one he used on policemen—and he thought they doubled both his fun and his income.

But none of it had cut any ice with Major March; he had never been beguiled by act, accent, proverbs, eyes or smiles. That might have been a simple matter of uncongenial personalities; it might have been because the Major preserved pheasants, and Dan was known to be the most diligent and artful poacher for miles in any direction. Dan's mother, whose appetite was finicky, could fancy a bit of roast pheasant as much as anything. The Major's pheasants were the fattest and tamest in the county. The Major knew it, and he knew Dan knew it. There was never a meeting of minds between them. The extensive gardens of Medwell Court were never incised by Dan's slow-moving spade; the joists of its numerous outbuildings were untouched by his leisurely hammer. He never earned a penny there. It was infuriating. Better luck next time? Dan was extremely interested to know who was buying the Court.

Everybody else in the neighbourhood was interested too, except old Mrs. Mallett, who was interested only in reclaiming her wayward son back from the ditches and dingles where he spent his scapegrace life, back into the bank in Milchester where he had once been such a promising young cashier. . . . Her arthritic hip was not greater pain to her than her only child's treachery. His father had been just the same. It was hard for her that there had been just two people important to her in her life, and she violently disapproved of both of them. It set her to grumbling; so did Dan's dogs, bantams and fancy pigeons. She took the same view of Dan as had Major March; as did P.C. Gundry, the village policeman; as did all the gamekeepers of a dozen parishes. Girls, by and large, took a different view.

The news broke, as news usually did, in the Chestnut Horse in the village. The talk in the bar had been about another of those explosions in an Indian restaurant. Seemed it was always happening. Quite a fuss there was in the papers, various theories put forward, all echoed in the bar of the Chestnut Horse. Indians and Chinese and such didn't properly understand gas; or Hindus were after the other lot; or it might be the National Front. Then old Denny Cobb, head gardener at the Court, came in with a bombshell larger, to the folk of Medwell Fratrorum, than any bang in an Indian restaurant. House and estate had found a buyer, after months of gradual reduction in the asking price.

The purchaser was a Mr Harold Dartie, who was or had been in business. He came from a south coast town, it might be Southampton or Portsmouth or Plymouth. He might be married. He might have children. He might be a gentleman farmer, and take the home farm in hand. He might be a sportsman, and fill the preserves with poults. He might be a local benefactor, giving jobs and handouts. He might be a hermit, a miser. His name was all that Denny Cobb actually knew. Denny's news was like a party balloon, appearing large but having only a fragment of substance. There was much speculation, then and there in the Chestnut Horse and in many places afterwards. Dan Mallett heard the speculation, joined in it (internally) and agreed that they must all just wait and see.

Medwell Court had stood empty for three months. Medwell Priory was almost empty for half the year—empty except for the caretakers during all the school holidays. It was an awful waste. Dan had, in fact, once or twice made use of attic dormitories and bathrooms, when the police were waiting for him in his cottage and other people were waiting for him elsewhere. He had felt like a pea in a drum—one small individual camping in those acres of rooms, avoiding, or failing to avoid, Jack and Ruby Collis, the caretakers. Jack and Ruby had just retired, none too soon—they were a nosey pair, forever disturbing a visitor's rest and interrupting his telephone calls in the headmistress's study—and there was a new couple stoking the boilers and keeping out tramps in the holidays. They were called Plummer; that, as in the case of Mr Harold Dartie, was all Dan knew about them. Nothing had recently taken Dan to the Priory; and if the Plummers did their shopping in the village, they did it when Dan was otherwise engaged.

And then, in June, still in the middle of the school's summer term, the first of the leaflets appeared in the window of the post office. They advertised something barely credible: something grandly called "The Medwell Summer Symposium of the Performing Arts." The Symposium was to be in August. It was to be held in and about the Priory. Perform-

5

ing artists, or artistes, were to perform to one another, each enriching the experience and so the interpretive powers of the others, each being so enriched. Cross-pollination was mentioned. It was hoped there would be actors, mimes, musicians of all kinds, singers, dancers, clowns and tumblers. Life would be simple but not comfortless. All meals were included in the overall fee, fresh and healthy country fare. It was to be a do-it-yourself sabbatical fortnight for all these gifted people—part of the fun would be sweeping, mopping, washing up; part of the total experience would be getting back to these basics of life.

Applications were to be addressed to the Organizing Secretary, Medwell Festival Society. Cheques were to be made out to the Society. For people who were going to do their own washing up, the fee seemed to Dan enormous. Imagination boggled at the whole thing. Nothing like it had ever occurred in the neighbourhood before. What kind of people came to such an affair? Earnest amateurs? Serious professionals? Beads and beards? Americans? Dimly Dan pictured clowns tumbling on the playing fields, actors declaiming in the dormitories, dancers twirling in the classrooms.

What it was all about, he concluded, was making profitable use of that great barrack of a building for a bit more of the year. He imagined he would see nothing of the Symposium.

Some of the women in the village, spelling out the leaflets in the post office window, went to ask for part-time jobs cleaning up after all those performing artists, who were probably untidy in their habits. But no staff was being taken on. There was nothing at all for the village, except possibly a bit of extra trade for pub, shop and garage. The local attitude to the Symposium therefore varied from apathetic to hostile. Dan, on balance, shared the apathy.

Fleets of expensive cars arrived at the Priory, and the little girls went away with their trunks. Then the teachers went

6

away in their little cars, the cleaners went away on their annual holidays, and only the caretakers were left.

A minibus came, with men and machinery. There was a great noise, as of a mighty wind, through the open windows of the Priory. The men were contract cleaners, come from a far place to make Medwell Priory fit for performing artists. The village was sore about that.

Vans came, and merchandise was unloaded under the supervision of a woman with short grey hair and red trousers. Dan, inconspicuous as a hedge-sparrow, watched this phase, the first that might have been of interest to him. It turned out not to be of much interest. The management of the Symposium had bought largely at a cash-and-carry—bulk purchases of such items as lavatory paper, ketchup, paper cups, tinned soup, liquid detergent. The woman in red trousers stayed when the vehicles went away, vanguard of the Symposium. From a distance, her manner seemed breezy and mannish; she looked as though she organised tours of museums, and stood no nonsense from the customers.

In the following few days she was joined by others, whom Dan observed simply because he had the habit of observation. (He was not himself observed; he had this habit too.) There was a spindly man, a burly woman, a young man with a beard, and a girl with thick spectacles who ran to and fro at the command of all the others. They were making ready for the Symposium. Dan wondered how you made ready for a Symposium; he could think of no preparations that made any sense at all.

The performing artists were due any day.

Vans were also busy at Medwell Court. Some painters had come and gone, but no major work like plumbing or wiring were being undertaken. All that had been done, recently and expensively; no doubt this was one of the attractions of the place to Mr Harold Dartie. The vans brought carpets and such. Dan, unseen, saw them going in, and heard the banging of tacks.

The arrival of objects at the Court interested him more than the arrival of performers at the Priory.

A man moved into Medwell Court who was evidently not Mr Harold Dartie. He revealed himself as an affable tough, in the post office and the pub, an ex-policeman now working in security. He was called Derek Davis, and he was there to guard Medwell Court and its contents until the owner arrived. It seemed that the insurance company had insisted on an arrangement which, to Dan, was odious. There was no secret about all this; on the contrary, Derek Davis's publicised occupation of the Court was an obvious deterrent to villains who might get ideas. It might be a serious deterrent to Dan. Dan inspected Derek Davis, from a corner of the bar of the Chestnut Horse. He was in his middle forties, ten or so years older than Dan. He was six-foot-plus. He would have tipped the scales at just about twice Dan's weight. He looked friendly and effective. He was not a man to tangle with. He fraternised immediately with Jim Gundry, the village policeman, legitimising his position, aligning himself with the local establishment. Dan wished him no ill; he just wished him a thousand miles away.

This view was not shared by the regulars of the Chestnut Horse, among whom Derek Davis became popular. Dan could see why, although he kept his own distance. The security man was gregarious and generous, and he had a lot of good stories.

Even though it was now guarded, Dan kept a discreet eye on the Court. He wanted to know where Derek Davis slept in the big house, and how deeply; and he wanted to know what goods and chattels were arriving.

Morally, Dan was purely the victim of circumstance. His mother's arthritis was no better. Her need for a hip operation was no less. Her refusal to go into the public ward of a National Health hospital remained granite. The cost of a private operation continued to rise. It seemed to Dan that every time he topped up his "deposit account"—the deepest of the rabbit holes in the Priory Woods—he was no more than keeping pace with inflation. A man who bought a place like Medwell Court would sure enough have silver that could be sold, informally, privately, to the firmly incurious antique dealer in Milchester. Dan did not feel that he was choosing, in the way of making a conscious and considered decision, to separate Mr Dartie from his silver. He was forced into doing so, by the lines of pain round his mother's mouth, by the ever-spiralling cost of the operation.

Like most houses with important gardens, Medwell Court had a large yew hedge, clipped to the smoothness of masonry. It divided the kitchen garden from the back courtyard. Dan, roosting in the middle of it, had a restricted but valuable view: he could see most of the back courtyard, the main back door (there were several subsidiary back doors) and the doors of several outbuildings. He could also, when the door was open, see a short way into the cavernous, stone-flagged back hall.

A pantechnicon arrived, a far larger vehicle than any which had brought carpets and lino and curtains. Its tailgate incorporated a fork-lift, which lowered crates onto a trolley. The crates went in through the back door on the trolley. Some of them carried large labels, with "GLASS" or "FRAG-ILE" stencilled in red. "Fragile," if not glass, meant china, porcelain, Wedgwood or Meissen or such: no good to Dan, really, considering the bumping about he'd be bound to give it. But crates unlabelled? Equally precious, it seemed, but not fragile? There might be books. Dan thought there was silver. The crates were laid in a row on the granite floor of the back hall.

Dan had a key to one of the other back doors of Medwell Court, the one that led into what they called the flower room. This dated from his relationship with the amiable Peggy Bowman, who had worked part-time as Major March's secretary.

9

Dan could borrow Fred Dawson's van, the back of which could hold a powerful quantity of silver. Fred wouldn't mind, because he wouldn't know about it. Dan had a key to the van.

The crates were nailed down. The lids could be jemmied off, but the nails coming out of the wood might make a right shriek. Derek Davis had made up a bed at the other end of the house; but with these new treasures arrived, he might put a camp bed in the back hall. Then he must be got away from the back hall. Dan would create a diversion—start a fire somewhere else in the house.

Speed was essential. If glass and porcelain and silver came, could Mr Harold Dartie be far behind?

Dan sat tight among the springy branches of the yew, planning his diversion, planning for all the contingencies he could think of, until the back door shut and the pantechnicon rolled away. Then he wriggled out of the garden, and loped out of the park, and retrieved his ancient bicycle from a forest of bracken. He bicycled home to give his mother her tea.

Passing Dave Sims's orchard, he saw that a new red flush was invading the polished skins of the apples. There was red in the hedges, of hips and haws and rowan berries. The harvest had hardly started; the sky blazed with midsummer heat; but these were the signs of the turn of the year. The drenching dews would be next, the milky mists over the water meadows, then the first frosts and the blankets of falling leaves: and then all his mother's miseries increased a hundredfold. The pain in her hip worse in the cold and damp; her temper no better; her beady-eyed inspection of his comings and goings getting sharper with age, rather than vaguer; her sense of betrayal at the way of life he had chosen growing more bitter rather than less, as she grew more helpless, more dependent.

His conscience pricked, Dan bicycled a little faster.

* * *

10

They had pigeon pie for supper—two wild cushat doves fat on Dave Sims's corn. The stock they were cooked in was enriched by a tumbler of claret. It was wine much too good for cooking, Dan knew; Sir George Simpson, who had paid for it, would have been greatly shocked. Sir George might not, perhaps, precisely have begrudged the wine to Dan; he had not precisely given it to him, either. Dan hoped the rich gravy on the dark, tender pieces of bird might tempt his mother's appetite. But she ate very little. Almost immobile, she could not do enough to give herself an appetite. It was heartbreaking. He looked at her with concern as she pushed her dinner about on her plate. She looked back at him with rage. She knew he was going out later. He did not know how she knew, but she always knew. Perhaps he betrayed some excitement, some alarm. It might be pleasure or business—a girl or a crock of gold; she might guess which, but Dan thought not. She would be curious, but too proud to ask. Certainly Dan would volunteer nothing. The less she knew, the better: not because she would betray any secret of his to anybody, but because suspicion of the way he spent his nights filled her with undiminishing fury. It couldn't be good for her, Dan thought, to be so angry; it couldn't help her sleep, or digest the little she had eaten.

Dan finished the claret he had not used in the cooking. He washed up and put everything away. He gave his dogs a run in the last of the daylight—Pansy the cross old pointer, Nimrod the great black lurcher greyhound, little Goldie the Jack Russell terrier. From the pigeon loft he heard the blue-laced Satinettes holding muffled, erotic conversations. The blue-marble bantams chuckled at him from the various places where they roosted.

He helped his mother to bed, up the crazy little stairs of the cottage. It was more and more wearisome for her, pulling herself by the banister, step after laborious step, her arthritic hand, like the claws of the bantams, clutching Dan's arm. When she was in bed he tucked her up. He drew back the scraps of curtain, and opened the window. She watched him from the pillow with eyes as sharp as an adder's. She would hear him go out. She was always a long, long time getting to sleep, and her senses were still as sharp as his own. She would lie in the dark, brooding about the life he might be living, the life he might be giving her. The bank. The neat suburban house. The dark suits, the briefcase, the respect of the community. Dan shuddered at her vision of the good life, and got ready for his visit to Medwell Court.

A young moon was setting when Dan crossed the country towards Fred Dawson's forge. He could see perfectly well; he hardly needed to see, because he knew his way so intimately. It was not a way anybody else would have chosen, but by night Dan used roads only in the cars he borrowed. On foot he went the fox's way, the badger's way, more direct and less conspicuous.

Fred's van was parked in its usual place behind the forge, invisible from the house even if there had been light to see by. Dan crept round the forge to the window of Fred's sitting room. The window was curtained, but through a crack in the curtains Dan saw a curiously garish light, and heard a voice with a false sound. Television. That was good. It was a quiet night, perfectly windless; even Fred and his dumpy wife might have heard the starter motor of the van.

The van started easily in the warm night air. Dan drove very slowly a little way without lights, in the last of the disappearing moonlight. He was in no hurry. He was wearing a thin black sweater, dark trousers, shoes with rubber soles, his old tweed cap, cotton gloves. He carried a flask, a pencil flash, a screwdriver and claw hammer for the crates, and his home-made blackthorn stick with the lump of lead in the handle.

It occurred to him, as he drove, that he should one day give Fred Dawson several gallons of petrol. But if he started giving petrol to all the people whose cars he borrowed, he would run the pumps dry, and that would be no favour to anybody.

His mental clock was striking one when he stopped the van three hundred yards from Medwell Court, pulling off the back drive and turning the van so that he could get away in a hurry. He had driven the last quarter mile very slowly and without lights. Derek Davis the security guard might be a light sleeper for professional reasons, as Dan himself was; he might be up and about for professional reasons, as Dan was. A thick belt of trees and the high wall of the kitchen garden intervened between his parking place and the house. Dan thought the muttering of his engine would hardly get through this insulation.

He sat in the van, looking and listening. There was no sound at all, of traffic, bird or bug. He put the screwdriver in the back pocket of his trousers. He carried the hammer. After a moment's thought he left his loaded blackthorn in the car. He did not at all intend to hit Derek Davis on the head, and if he had to do something so uncongenial the hammer would serve.

He went through the door in the garden wall, leaving it ajar. He went very slowly, silently, down the cinder path between the runner beans and lettuces which Denny Cobb was growing for himself. His eyes were becoming every moment more used to the darkness.

Outside the back courtyard a van was parked, facing down the back drive. It was not the pantechnicon which had delivered the crates, nor any of the vans which had brought carpets and the other stuff. It was puzzling. Derek Davis had not a van but a Ford Fiesta. Was the driver of this van staying in the house? If not, where was he? Was he a friend of Derek Davis, an unauthorised houseguest? Were these security reinforcements, called for by the value of the crates? That was a thoroughly unwelcome idea. In the thin darkness Dan saw that the van's side was boldly lettered: "ACME VAN HIRE—SELF-DRIVE." Not the security company. There

13

might be a lot of reasons why a personal friend of Derek Davis had come to relieve his loneliness in a self-drive van, but if that was the explanation, why was the van parked so far from the house? Why not right outside the back door?

Dan crept up to the van, a newish Bedford. There was nothing in it, front or back. It was not locked. The key was in the ignition.

The explanation came to Dan, so obvious that he was astonished he had not thought of it at once. Somebody else was on the same errand as he was. Had someone else, from another hiding place, seen the crates arrive? No. Dan was hypersensitive to the presence of other people, other furtive watchers; he knew he had had the yew hedge to himself. Then a bent employee of the removals firm had tipped off a villain that valuable stuff was being delivered to an almost empty house. Something like that. It happened all the time. Losing no more time than Dan had, the villain was here, his van outside the courtyard and, like Dan's, pointing the right way for a quick departure. Did the villain know about Derek Davis? If not, what would he do about it when he found out? Was Derek Davis in the game too? Dan thought not, though objectively it was an obvious possibility.

If any of this was right, Dan was in for a more complicated night than he had expected. Not necessarily a less profitable one. It depended how things worked out. Making a first effort to influence how things worked out, Dan took the ignition key out of the Bedford's dashboard.

Moving like a slow-motion spider, Dan prowled into the back courtyard. The first thing he saw confirmed that his guess had been right. An extension ladder was leaning against the wall of the house, near the main back door where the crates had gone in. The top of the ladder rested beside an upstairs window. The window was wide open, the lower section pushed up behind the upper. Dan imagined that one of the panes of the lower section was broken; the burglar had reached in and opened the catch. Probably, for the sake of quiet, the burglar had used a glass cutter and a piece of putty. Even so, Derek Davis ought to have heard him. And he ought to hear the lids being jemmied off the crates.

Was Derek Davis away for the night? Was that possible? Was it another thing the burglar had been tipped off about? Dan knew where the security man kept his Fiesta, in one of the garages off the back courtyard. The evening might, after all, be turning out simple. But the Fiesta was there, in an unlocked garage but itself locked. The house was guarded, then. Dan wondered again: did the burglar know? What was he proposing to do about it, if he did know, and how would he react if suddenly discovered?

Dan had had an excellent plan for dealing with Derek Davis, involving creating a diversion, by remote control, in the coal cellar. That plan was obsolete. Perhaps the other intruder would provide the diversion. All sorts of possibilities presented themselves. Dan could prepare only by being prepared for anything.

Listening hard, moving like a shadow, Dan prowled round to the side of the house and to the small door of which Peggy Bowman had, long before, irresponsibly given him the key.

The key turned easily. He opened the door, swinging it no faster than the hour hand of a clock. He slipped in, leaving the door ajar behind him. It was pitch dark. There was no sound from anywhere. Presumably the burglar had not yet started jemmying the lids from the crates. Dan wanted to be nearby when he did start. It was a job he was hoping was going to be done for him.

Dan risked a blink from his pencil flash. A stone-flagged passage led out of the flower room. There was a corner with two other doors, which gave to gun rooms, boot rooms or such. You turned right to get to the back hall. Dan crept along the passage to the corner, his fingertips on the wall on his right, so that he could steer without seeing, his hammer in his left hand. At the corner he stopped, and looked, and listened. The back hall was a cavern of utter blackness, utter

15

silence. All the crates were there, where they had been put in a row nine hours before.

No light. No jemmying of lids.

Had Dan missed the bus? Had the burglar come and gone with all the silver? No—his transport was still there.

How many burglars? With how many guns?

Dan crept along the remaining yards of the passage, to the arch which gave onto the back hall. He was ready to bolt back to the corner. As he reached the arch he heard voices. He froze, flattened to the wall. There were two voices, men, upstairs, on the landing of the back stairs. There was a glow of light from the landing, its source invisible. Two burglars, or a burglar and Derek Davis. Dan strained to hear what they said. A deep voice seemed to be giving orders. A lighter voice seemed to be protesting, arguing, maybe pleading. Dan thought the lighter voice was Derek Davis. The light strengthened. It was a big flash, in the hand of someone who was approaching the top of the stairs. A figure appeared at the top of the stairs, silhouetted against the glow of light on the white-painted wall behind him. A big, powerful man. Tousled hair. Dressing gown and pyjamas. Derek Davis. Not talking now; standing silent with his back to the stairs.

There was a loud explosion, the crack of a gun, which reverberated in the cavern of staircase and hall. There were two more shots in rapid succession. Derek Davis was knocked over backwards. He rolled untidily down the stairs, coming to rest with his feet on the bottom step. His position was crumpled, unnatural. Dan was sure he was dead.

A man came down the stairs, his face and gun invisible behind the flashlight.

16

2

THE MURDERER shone the torch at the body. With his toe he lifted a shoulder and dropped it. He satisfied himself that his victim was dead.

Derek Davis was an undignified corpse, the more pathetic for having his head on the floor and his legs up the stairs, for wearing pyjamas and dressing gown.

Dan shrank back along the passage and round the corner. The murderer's gun was in his pocket, but it could come out pretty quickly. He had fired three times. It was a good idea to assume that there were plenty of rounds left in the magazine in the automatic's handgrip. This was a man who did not mind shooting people.

Dan felt stunned and a little sick. This was not a person being blackmailed and driven by despair into murdering his blackmailer; not a husband whose wife had been stolen driven by jealousy into killing her paramour. This was a man so greedy that he killed, in cold blood, a decent and honourable man, middle-aged, father of a family, who got in his way.

Dan surprised himself, feeling like that about an ex-policeman whom he had hardly known; but the words had come into his head unbidden, and they were the right words.

The murderer went to the back door. His flash went up one side of the door and down the other. He found the light switch, and used it. The back hall was flooded with harsh white light from an overhead bulb in a glass shade. The windows each side of the door were shuttered; any light that filtered out would be visible only from the back courtyard.

Light washed down the passage through the arch, with diminishing brightness. Dan dropped to his knees. He would be very difficult to see, peeping round the corner, from the glare in the hall; he would be the more difficult to see the closer he was to the ground.

The murderer turned from the door and walked towards the crates. Like Dan's, his shoes had rubber soles. There was a tiny squeak each time he put one of his feet down on the stones of the floor. His shoe soles were the only things about him liable to squeak. He looked hard, a wooden man with a wooden face. There should have been some expression on those white-wood features, since he had put three bullets into the chest of a fellow creature half a minute before. Dan would have expected a show of grief, glee, fear, shock, something. There was no expression at all. The man had performed a necessary task, perhaps tiresome, perhaps even a little repugnant, like unblocking a drain, or putting a mouse out of its misery, and he had dismissed it from his mind while he addressed himself to more important matters.

He was a little over six foot; aged about fifty; solid without massiveness; his face untanned in spite of the time of the year; his pepper-and-salt hair cut short and brushed straight back from his brow. He had a square jaw and a broad, thin-lipped mouth. He moved stiffly. Dan understood the reason when he pulled a crowbar from his trouser leg.

He made short work of the lids of two of the crates; he left alone those marked "GLASS" and "FRAGILE." He made a lot of noise. He was not worried about noise.

Dan had guessed right. It was silver.

There was not as much, in quantity, as the size of the

18

crates suggested, because there was a lot of packing material. Straw, crumpled newspaper and what looked like kapok spread itself over the flagstones. The silver had to be valuable indeed to have been so extensively padded. The pieces were individually wrapped in tissue paper. The murderer unwrapped each one enough to see what it was, then wrapped it up again and put it on one of the unopened crates. His movements were deliberate, unhurried. He treated the silver with respect. It was evident to Dan that he knew what he was about.

From the floor beyond the crates he picked up some canvas bags, capacious but folding flat. Obviously he had brought them with him. He packed the silver, in its tissue paper, into the bags, putting in some of the padding also.

It was just half past two, Dan thought, when all the silver had been packed into the five canvas bags.

The murderer opened the back door. He was not worried about anybody seeing the light. Almost certainly nobody would; anybody who did would assume that the security man was on patrol.

Dan assumed he would go to his van, intending to back it up to the door. What would he do when he found the key missing? Guess right? Or think he had taken it out of the dash? Search the van for it, search his pockets for it, eventually search the house for it?

But the murderer was not bothering to move the van. He picked up four of the canvas bags by their leather handles, and went out with them. He carried them as though they were weightless.

It was time for Dan to move. The murderer would not discover about the key until all five bags were in the van. When he did discover, Dan wanted to be as near the van as possible. He made sure he had the key safe in his hip pocket.

Dan was halfway across the flower room when the door which he had left ajar swung wide. At the same instant the room's overhead light snapped on. Dan was face to face with

19

the murderer, eight feet away. There was a frozen moment—a fraction of a second of utter amazement. They simply stood and stared at one another, rigid as dolls, for that fraction of a second. Then the murderer's hand flew to the bulging pocket of his coat, and Dan turned and fled. He was barely round the corner when he heard the crash of the pistol. He was across the back hall and out of the door when it crashed again, from the corner. He imagined he could feel the wind of the bullet's passing.

Dan's intimate local knowledge, as so often before, was his salvation. The back courtyard, the jumble of outbuildings, the yew hedge, the kitchen garden. A single stranger would never have caught him, even by daylight. He moved like a bat, like a field mouse. The beam of the big torch stabbed the darkness and swept paths, gates, hedges, outbuildings. It was being used intelligently and dangerously. Beside it was the gun. Dan made a wide circuit, arriving on the back drive fifty yards from the Bedford van. He crawled up the side of the drive towards the van. He found, to his surprise, that he was still holding his hammer. Since he had brought it so far he held on to it. He lay under a bush, ten yards from the van, considering his next move. The murderer had stopped pounding about and waving his torch. He was watching and waiting. Where? Obviously he was watching the van. His eyes, without the dazzle of the torch beam, would be getting used to the darkness.

Dan tried to put himself in the murderer's shoes. Where would he be? In front of the van or behind it, so that he could watch both doors. Behind it rather than in front, so that he could watch the rear door. Also because the doors hinged at the front so that, open, they provided a kind of shield against a bullet coming from the front. Dan expected the murderer to be in the mouth of the back courtyard, some ten yards directly behind the van. That was where he ought to be. Dan hoped he had the common sense to do what Dan chose for him to do.

20

Dan waited, not much liking the immediate future. It was only a few minutes since the last of the silver had gone into the last canvas bag, which was still, unfortunately, in the back hall. There was time, but not unlimited time. It would not do to be lying under the bush at dawn. There was a great deal to be done, with van and silver and necessary travelling.

The murderer was as patient as Dan was. He could hold just as still.

Both sides held important cards. The other had a gun and a powerful flashlight; Dan had the key of the van.

Dan had his hammer. It had seemed supremely useless in this situation; suddenly, and obviously, it was supremely useful. A fair-sized stone or a half brick would have served, but no such things were lying about in this impeccable estate. The hammer was anyway much better.

Slowly, slowly, Dan extricated himself from his bush. Slowly he rose to his feet behind it. He swung the hammer, two full circles, with his arm straight. He released it. It soared away into the darkness. He had very little idea where it would land. It seemed to spend an hour in the air. Dan waited like a sprinter on his blocks. There was a moderate crash. The hammer landed somewhere on the cobbles of the courtyard. There was an immediate shot, and the torch beam came on and darted about the courtyard. Dan was at the passenger's door of the van. He went in like a snake, keeping below the level of the seat backs. From the tail of his eye he saw that the rear door of the van was open. Obviously it would be; it was something he had forgotten to expect. It increased the unpleasantness of the position. After an agony of fumbling, he slotted the ignition key into the dash. He wondered if the engine needed choking; he wondered where the choke was. Almost lying along the seats, he gulped and turned the key. The engine fired. He put the van into gear (any gear), released the hand brake, and put his foot down. The gun roared behind him, again and again. A bullet thudded into the dashboard. The windscreen shattered. He rocketed down the back drive, swerving. If there were more shots, the roar of the engine drowned them.

When he turned out into the road he remembered Fred Dawson's van. Something might have to be done about that; but not yet.

He stopped, and closed the rear of the van. He confirmed that the four canvas bags were there. He regretted his hammer, which was a good one, and which he had actually paid money for.

He drove on, asking himself what had happened, how that mind-freezing confrontation had happened.

The murderer had taken the four bags out to the van. He either then decided to move the van, or checked that the key was in the ignition. He must have concluded that he had taken the key out of the dash. He must have searched his pockets; then retraced his steps. Presumably he had a pocket flash as well as the big one. Retracing his steps had taken him to Dan's door; either he had made a precautionary circuit of the house, or he had tried all the outside doors on the off chance of one being unlocked. Coming to Dan's door he had seen it was ajar. So in he went. Perhaps not exactly like that, but something like that.

Who the murderer was Dan might never know. Very likely he came from the same south coast city as Mr Harold Dartie. He thus either knew about, or was tipped off about, Mr Dartie and his silver and his move. Possibly he knew, from one of the men who delivered the crates, where Derek Davis bunked; possibly Derek Davis caught him breaking in by that upstairs window.

He probably assumed Dan came from the same place he did, and had the same sort of sources of information.

Part of Dan wanted to go immediately to the police, with the excellent description of the murderer he could give them. He was so astonished at himself that he almost went into the ditch. The idea only had to be examined to be discarded. He was not keen to admit that he had entered Medwell Court, feloniously, at two in the morning. He was not keen to surrender the silver he had risked his life to get.

He decided that if Mr Harold Dartie was a very nice man, he would give him some of his silver back. Perhaps all of it. For the moment, it was better in a rabbit hole.

Into a rabbit hole in the Priory Woods it went; and by four in the morning no human eye, and not many dogs' noses, could have told that anything was there.

As Dan drove towards Milchester, he was struck by another thought he should have had a long time before. The murderer would assume that Dan had arrived in a vehicle. He would look for the vehicle. He would find Fred Dawson's van at dawn if not long before. Presumably he would drive it back to wherever he came from; or possibly to a railway station. That solved the problem of Fred's van, though not in a way quite convenient to Fred.

Presumably the people who owned the self-drive Bedford would put out a call for it, maybe within hours, maybe not for a fortnight, depending how long it had been hired for, if it had been legitimately hired. There might be bullets lodged in it, which might be found. They might be matched up to the bullets in Derek Davis. That would link the van to the murderer; it would identify the murderer only if he had neglected the most obvious precautions.

Dan supposed the murderer would take his consolation prize, the fifth and final bag. If this made him a little less angry it would only be a very little. He was a man Dan was anxious never to see again. Dan would stay away from the south coast, to which in any case nothing drew him.

Dan drove through Milchester to the station at the far end of the town. He drove into the station car park, which was almost empty. He backed the van against the wall of a warehouse at the far end of the car park, to hide any bullet holes there might be. The broken windscreen was just a broken windscreen.

He looked about for his home-made blackthorn. He re-

23

membered he had left it in Fred Dawson's van. He had made a present of it to the murderer. He was unreasonably angry about this.

The murderer had made Dan a present too, besides the four bags of silver, which Dan only discovered in his idiotic search for the blackthorn. On the floor in front of the passenger's seat was a briefcase: the stiff, executive, foursquare kind, in black leather, resembling a miniature suitcase, and for all Dan knew used as one by the kind of man his mother wanted him to be.

His hands still gloved, Dan examined the briefcase in the dim light coming from the empty and silent station.

Gold initials stamped on the top: H.F.D. The murderer's initials. No, no—committing the kind of crime Dan had just seen did not go with owning a personalized executive briefcase. Stolen, then. If so, it provided not the slightest link to the murderer. Or only a very tenuous link. It was possible that if he stole a man's briefcase, he came from the same place as that man. It was just barely possible that the owner of the briefcase might know or suspect who had stolen it. It might give the bluebottles some tiny kind of clue. So the thing was to leave the briefcase in the van. No. It might once again get stolen before the van was found. The thing was to leave it by Derek Davis's body. Assuming, to be sure, that the murderer was well away by then.

The briefcase was unlocked. It was being used—or had been, by its owner, H.F.D.—as both briefcase and mini-suitcase. There were a shirt and a tie, the shirt a decent cotton one with small checks, the tie silk with a foulard pattern. Nob's clothes. There was a toothbrush, a tube of dentifrice, an electric shaver. There was a small address book, loose-leafed with a ring binder, the addresses typed. The names were foreign, exotic, Greek and Indian and Chinese; or they were names like "Raj" or "Bombay" or "Wall of China"; or they said "Curry House" or "Takeaway." The addresses were mostly in the large towns of the south coast, Plymouth,

Torquay, Bournemouth, Southampton, Portsmouth. Dan thought they were all restaurants, using the word in its widest sense. It was the address book of a man who liked foreign food. No. Of a man who sold ketchup or knives or kitchen equipment, or who inspected catering premises for the Ministry of Health.

There was at the bottom of the case a file cover incorporating a clip. There was correspondence addressed to H. F. Dartie, Esq., at an address in Weymouth, and carbon copies of his replies. The correspondence was with an insurance company and a security firm. It included a recent valuation of a collection of antique silver.

Everything was immediately and totally explained. The murderer had stolen the briefcase, on a train or out of a parked car, expecting maybe a gold pencil or a couple of credit cards. What he got was an inventory of a valuable collection of silver, the date on which it would arrive at its new home, the precise location of that home, and the identity and description of the security man who was being posted to guard it. An engraved invitation to commit robbery, which would almost inevitably involve murder.

Mr Dartie would rue his carelessness, and so would his insurance company, and so would Derek Davis's wife and children.

There was still a thin possibility that Mr Harold Dartie might have an idea who had stolen his briefcase—might have glimpsed a big man with a pale face and stiff pepper-and-salt hair running away down a station platform or across a car park. That the briefcase might, therefore, point the bluebottles in the right direction.

Dan borrowed a bicycle from the rack outside the station, issuing sincere mental apologies to the night-shift worker who had left it there. He pedalled away slowly, the briefcase strapped to the carrier behind the saddle. It was altogether too far to bicycle at that time of night, but it would have been folly to leave the van anywhere nearer home.

25

The sky began to pale as he went.

Two and three months earlier, the countryside would have been brimful of birdsong under this whitening sky. Now most of the birds were silent; after nesting and breeding and rearing, they felt no need of song, for attracting mates or for asserting ownership of territory. Dan was grateful for the few exceptions: the gentle warble of the greenfinch's number-two song, the yellowhammer's unvarying demand for a little bit of bread and no cheese, the dying fall of the willow wren. That one would be away south soon, with the swallows and the rest. Dan wished he could turn his mother into a migrant bird, so that she could warm her old bones all winter in a dry African sun.

Dan was feeling bottomlessly weary when he pedalled more slowly than ever up the back drive of the Court. He dismounted and leaned the bicycle on the far side of a bush. There was just a chance that the murderer, lingering for some unguessable reason, would take Fred Dawson's van down the drive and see a bicycle in his headlights.

Prowling up the drive with the briefcase, Dan saw that Fred Dawson's van had gone. Taking the murderer, taking Dan's blackthorn, taking the fifth bag of silver.

Dan wondered if anything in the briefcase was good to him. The valuation of the silver, to strengthen his hand in negotiations with the incurious proprietor of the Box of Delights in Milchester ("Highest Prices Paid for Unwanted Silver")? No. That was asking the lady to be too blatantly a receiver of stolen goods, and anyway Dan knew he had to be brave about accepting rock-bottom prices. The shirt? Far too big for him. The tie? A foulard-patterned silk tie could play no conceivable useful role in Dan's life. The electric razor? Dan preferred soap and water. The address book? Dan stopped, opened the briefcase, and pocketed the address book, without the slightest idea why he was doing so. He was almost too tired to think.

Although he was now sure that the big house was tenanted only by the pathetic, undignified corpse of Derek Davis, Dan approached it stealthily. The lights that had blazed in the back hall were off. The ladder was still against the wall and the upstairs window open. The door into the flower room was shut but not locked.

Using his pencil flash, Dan put the briefcase behind one of the crates marked "FRAGILE." The bluebottles would find it. They would do the same sums that Dan had done. They would conclude that in all the excitement of stealing and killing, the murderer had forgotten it. Or run away in a panic. Or even that he had no further use for it.

Going out as softly as he had come in, Dan locked the flower-room door behind him. That was very necessary. Peggy Bowman knew he had the key because she had given it to him. She wouldn't want to betray him, but murder was murder, and if she was asked outright how somebody came to have a key to that door, she might feel obliged to say. So it was better that the question never arose, and it was assumed that the murderer had come and gone by the ladder.

Dan retrieved his borrowed bicycle, and rode it to the Chestnut Horse in the village. He put the bicycle in the yard behind the pub. There were usually a few there. Blokes went away at closing time forgetting they'd come on their bikes; or somebody gave them a lift; or they knew they'd fall off if they tried to ride home. One or two of the bicycles, Dan thought, had been there for years. The owner might get this one back. Dan thought not. Nobody in Medwell would know it had come from Milchester; nobody in Milchester would know it had gone to Medwell.

Dan walked the last leg of his journey, almost too tired to do so.

At noon, refreshed by five hours' sleep and a gigantic breakfast, Dan went into the village on his own bicycle. He did a bit of shopping, and went to the Chestnut Horse.

The murder was out. Iris Chandler, who went up to the

Court to Hoover the floors—only twice a week, now it was empty—had found the body at nine o'clock. She was holding court now in the Chestnut Horse. Her grief was genuine—she had actually liked that Mr. Davis—but her glory was genuine too, and so were the brown ales she was bought. The telephone having been cut off, she had locked up the door again and bicycled at top speed to the village and to P.C. Gundry. It was difficult to imagine Iris Chandler bicycling at top speed, but it was easy to imagine Jim Gundry telephoning at top speed. By now the Court would be swarming with policemen, fingerprinters, photographers, doctors, and probably that chief detective superintendent, all too well known to Dan, who gave his character away by looking like a fox.

Mr Dartie had been sent for, because of the burglary. The insurance people were coming too.

Beside these dramas, the disappearance of Fred Dawson's van was a minor item. Even Fred saw that his van was not headline news. For a moment it looked as though it might be—someone suggested that Fred's van must have been the murderer's getaway car. The spotlight swung towards Fred. But opinion in the Chestnut Horse swung it back again: If the burglar and murderer came from far away, how did he get to Fred Dawson's? And if he was a local man, where was the van now? It was a yob on the run from Borstal who'd nicked a lot of car keys; he'd drive it till he ran out of petrol, then leave it in a lay-by. By now all the police everywhere would have the number and description of the van. Fred would get it back. If not, he was insured.

A replacement arrived to guard Medwell Court, at four o'clock that same day. In background he was identical to Derek Davis, in manner more taciturn. It seemed a case of shutting the stable door after the horse had been stolen, but there was valuable stuff, they said, in the other crates, and more stuff arriving very soon.

The ladder had been taken down and locked away, after

28

the police had tested it for fingerprints. It was too much of an invitation, leaning there against the house, to a tramp or a lad out of work.

Next morning, after the police gave their go-ahead, the broken pane in the upstairs window was replaced. The man brought his own ladder, and took it away with him.

The national press carried small items about the murder, the local press large ones. There was speculation about how the violent robber had known about the crates of silver in the almost empty house. A theory was that he came from Mr Dartie's home town, and thus knew about his movements and his treasures. Another theory—not necessarily in contradiction—was that the beast had been tipped off, possibly by an employee of the removals firm, possibly by innocent idle chatter in a pub or on a bus. It was thought that the police were working on these lines.

Hearing these theories in the Chestnut Horse, Dan realised that the police were keeping quiet about the briefcase. They had undoubtedly found it, unless Iris Chandler had pinched it, which was not probable. What the police were actually doing, Dan thought, was pursuing lines of investigation following his own train of thought when he planted the briefcase in the Court; they were hoping Mr Dartie might have an idea who stole his briefcase; and they were doing all this in secret so as not to alert the murderer. At least, Dan hoped that was what was happening, and he hoped it worked.

He wondered what Mr Dartie—now, presumably, with his briefcase restored to him—made of the disappearance of the address book. Dan was still not sure why he had taken it. It was hidden in his cottage. There might someday be some use for it.

Mr Dartie had arrived. He was staying at the Red Lion, once a coaching inn, now the one pretentious hotel in Milchester. He could not yet move into his own grand new resi-

29

dence, as it had no furniture except for the few sticks Derek Davis had used. Besides, it was going to be full of policemen for a few days yet. It seemed that he had not turned against the house by reason of a murder having just been committed in it. The village was agog for a sight of him.

The first of the Symposium's customers arrived, observed with mild curiosity by Dan. These exotics would have aroused wider interest, but for the sensational events at the Court. As it was, they were hardly noticed.

Two arrived together in a little car; one on a bicycle with saddlebags; some in taxis from Milchester station. Some thirty were expected. It seemed the Symposium was undersubscribed. Next year it would be altogether bigger and better.

The people looked like people, to Dan's disappointment. He had expected freaks, but they were only freakish in doing something so weird as spending a lot of money to do their own washing up in an empty girls' school. They looked old, serious and dull. Though old, the men tended to blue denim jackets that looked like prison uniforms; though old, the women tended to garments of an ethnic or peasant character, with wooden beads and rope-soled slippers. Dan wondered what they all performed. He did not think they were acrobats, tumblers, ballet dancers, stand-up comics or opera singers. He did not want to see or hear their performances.

Then the girl arrived, abruptly changing his whole attitude to the Symposium.

She came in a big new car, with a tall woman of about fifty. She was not tall, and she was about twenty-two. The tall woman had a commanding manner and a ringing baritone voice. Carrying over the gravel to the shrubbery where Dan was roosting, the voice communicated that the woman was American. This suggested that the girl was also American. Dan had never met an American girl; he immediately and badly wanted to meet this one. She wore yellow cotton pants and a shirt of blue and white checks. These summer clothes revealed, while they concealed, the sort of figure Dan liked best. Her dark hair was cropped short. Her face and arms were tanned. Her features, from a distance, looked small, neat, friendly. She jumped out of the car with the exuberance of a child, and began pulling a lot of cases out of the back. She was active; she was stronger than she looked, unless the cases were empty.

Was she a customer? A performing artist? What did she perform? Dan wanted to be there.

The directorate of the Symposium came out of the house to greet the Americans, as well as some other people who were also arriving. The girl and her companion were swallowed up into the crowd and into the house. Dan wished he was a customer. He thought that, in the words of the Symposium's prospectus, he would be enriched in all kinds of ways. Could he give a performance? Much of his life was devoted to giving performances, but not, perhaps, of the kind the Symposium called for.

A girl like that wouldn't be cooped up indoors, not in weather like this, not all the time. He wouldn't have to gate-crash the Symposium; merely lurk. It would take a good deal of time, but time was a thing he could arrange to have plenty of.

Dan went to the Chestnut Horse early in the evening. There was a car he did not recognise, parked outside the pub. Ted Goldingham, the landlord, was talking to a stranger across the bar. The stranger had his back to Dan. He was a big man, well dressed in a lightweight worsted suit, with very shiny brown brogues. He and Ted were talking about the murder of Derek Davis; Ted was saying what a shame it was, a family man and only doing his duty. The stranger agreed heartily. He had a strong, deep voice, almost a gentleman's voice. It struck a chord of memory in Dan.

The stranger half turned, so that Dan could see his face. Dan knew him. It was a face he would never forget.

Dan slid back out of the door, his heart pounding. He did

31

not think the stranger had seen him. He devoutly hoped not. The stranger was the man who had killed Derek Davis.

Dan waited for the stranger to leave the pub, himself inconspicuously lounging where he could see the silver BMW.

The stranger was only another twenty minutes. He went away in his beautiful, powerful car. Dan made sure he really did go away. He went off in the direction of Milchester. Dan waited a little longer, in case he came back for his hat.

"Speak of the devil," said Ted Goldingham. "Just bin talkin' about you. Bloke wants an odd-job man he can call on at short notice, for patchin' his sheds an' such. So I give him your name. An' I said I'd be seein' you, an' I'd tell you to go an' see him. I reckon I done you a favour."

"But who?"

"I'm tellin' you. Was in here jus' now."

"That stranger? The tall bloke?"

"Not a stranger no longer."

"But who is he?"

"Why, you are be'ind the times, ruddy Dan Mallett. I thought you knew everything before it happened. He's bin all over the village all afternoon, doin' the civil with everybody. Dr Smith an' the Vicar an' such. That's our new squire, so to say. That's Mr Harold Dartie, jus' bought the Court an' had his silver pinched."

3

"THEY'RE MOVIN' IN the big stuff day after tomorrow," said
Ted Goldingham over the beer mats. "Meantime he's stop-
pin' here. Prob'ly here a week or ten days. More on the spot
than Milchester. Just off to get his stuff. Be back any minute.
You wait here for him, an' you can meet him straight off."

"Hum," said Dan. "Mother's tea's overdue already. I'd
best shift."

Dan sped out of the village, startling the people who saw
him. He was used to bicycling very slowly. He disliked ped-
alling at speed, not because it was tiring or undignified, but
because it inhibited his observation of the world round him.
He liked checking up in the village, as well as in the countryside—people's gardens, their new front-room curtains, any
unfamiliar cars, as well as the progress through the seasons
of the smaller, quieter creatures of the hedges and ditches.
But he was disinclined to be seen even at a great distance by
Mr Harold Dartie.

Dan had a first, fleeting hope that Ted Goldingham had
got it wrong. The murderer had come back to the village
confident that nobody there had seen him except one small

criminal who had probably himself come from far away. He might have any number of reasons for coming, such as looking for four out of five bags of antique silver. He said he was Harold Dartie, in order to get the entrée everywhere, to get everyone talking freely to him, knowing that none of them had seen the real Dartie, that he was far away. . . .

It didn't do. Harold Dartie had gone straight to the Court, the times he came to look at it, with the estate agents. But people must have seen him. Nobody would take such an absurd risk as Dan's first theory required.

It had to be faced, then. The man with the grim jaw, the thin mouth, the pepper-and-salt hair, the freely used automatic pistol, was the new owner of Medwell Court.

Stealing his own silver? Why not? Other people had done it. Edwin Calloway of the Woodbines had lost a bit of silver to Dan, but nothing like as much as he claimed for from the insurance. He'd stolen the rest from himself, years before, sold it, and left it on the insurance schedule. The more money you started with, the easier it was to make money. Dan thought Harold Dartie had not started with a lot, but he had, in the course of some career or other, come by a lot. And he'd hoped to come by a lot more, by staging that phony burglary and killing Derek Davis. He still would come by a lot of insurance money, but he'd expected to have both money and silver. That was completely obvious. It was a sneaky sort of carry-on, but it was understandable.

Derek Davis was something else. He was there on Dartie's instructions. If it was the insurance company's idea, still Dartie would have known about it. Almost certainly he would have met Derek Davis, briefed him about the house, the valuables, told him where he could sleep and how he could cook. Dartie must by now have keys. He had gone in through an upstairs window to make it all look like an outside job. Making a noise. Knowing Derek Davis was there, that he'd hear, that he'd come. Ready for that, with his big automatic full of bullets.

34

All of that must be about right. It followed that Harold Dartie came to the Court fully prepared to murder Derek Davis, fully intending to do so. A man he knew, his own employee who trusted him.

It was hardly credible, but it had to be believed.

It was possible, Dan supposed, that Dartie had a grudge against Derek Davis, that he wanted to kill him anyway. Maybe something had happened when Derek Davis was still a policeman. Dartie was killing two birds with one stone, with one bullet. It made no difference to Dan's position.

Which looked worse, the more Dan examined it.

Harold Dartie had been making himself known in pub, post office, vicarage, surgery. Which suggested he intended to be *that* kind of local magnate—popular, pulling his weight, familiar figure, bluff and friendly, part of the scene. Reading the lesson in church, president of the cricket club and the flower show.

Knowing everybody in sight.

If Dan went about his usual business, it would be days rather than weeks, hours rather than days, before Harold Dartie saw him. Who's that little horror coming out of the post office? Dan Mallett, they all cry, anxious to be seen to be helpful to the popular new squire. Lives with his old mam by the Priory Woods. We can show you his cottage, Mr Dartie, sir. He's the biggest villain unhung, for all he's so small.

Dan thought of the cold-blooded killing at the top of Mr Dartie's own back stairs.

He thought of his hostages to fortune—his mother, almost helpless with arthritis; his dogs, beloved beyond any computation of their value; his laboriously bred Satinettes, and his confiding blue-marble bantams with the feathery trousers. . . .

Dan couldn't suddenly become a hermit. He had to go into the village. He had to go to the post office to buy things and the pub to hear things. He had to go to the various gardens where he pruned and the houses where he hammered. He could go to ground for a little while, but only a very little while. He needed some money to live, and a lot of money for the operation; and his mother could only be left alone to look after herself for a very few days at a time.

Going right away would solve nothing. Harold Dartie wasn't going to go away. The problem would be there until it was removed.

There was this about it too—Dan's absence would be noticed. Not for a day or two, perhaps, but pretty briskly. People whose gardens he pretended to dig would compare notes. Where's Dan? Has anyone seen that wretched Mallett? Word gets to Harold Dartie, from a gardener or a housemaid or Ted Goldingham or a nob he's giving a drink to. Dan Mallett, eh? Disappeared, eh? What kind of bloke? Biggest villain unhung, eh? Little scruffy bloke with blue eyes. Ah. And his old mother lives in that cottage there. Ah.

There was even this about it—Harold Dartie was expecting Dan to report himself at the Court with his hammer and his screwdriver and his paintbrush.

Only he'd left his best hammer on the cobblestones of the Court's back yard. . . .

It seemed to Dan that he had to keep out of Harold Dartie's sight, while keeping Harold Dartie in sight. He had to find a way of neutralising Harold Dartie, without getting himself neutralised. The latter would happen if he let himself be seen by Dartie, or suspected of burglary by the police.

How did you neutralise a big, rich, successful, dangerous, trigger-happy man like Dartie?

By killing him. In some ways best all round, but not a serious proposition to Dan. By exposing him to the police, in such a way that Dan's own part in the night's frolic was not also exposed. That was a serious proposition, all right, but suffered from the disadvantage that it was impossible.

Supposing it to be possible, it meant staying nearby,

which might be bad for Dan's health but would be good for his mother's. Staying in hiding from which he could emerge at short notice, while remaining hidden even though he had emerged.

Cobwebs festooned the hedgerows, another sign of autumn. Dan slowed to look at them. He marvelled, as so often before, at the industry and artistry of the spinners; he marvelled that devices so ruthlessly lethal were so dainty and decorative. A big cobweb spanned a gap between branches, almost brushing Dan's face as he rode; in the middle of it a small brown fly was struggling. There was no sign of the spider. There would be.

Mr Harold Dartie was a very large and predatory spider who had just bought a very large and expensive cobweb. Dan was a little brown fly struggling in the middle of the cobweb. The spider had not yet spotted him. How long did Dan have? Supposing that he had a few days, what was he going to do with them?

Dan's mind began going round and round, and in his preoccupation he bicycled slower and slower. He bicycled so slowly that he wobbled and almost fell off. He went a little faster, just enough to maintain equilibrium—and decided that he faced a chain of unresolvable paradoxes. He surprised himself with this pompous phrase, which had surfaced like a fat trout from the depths of his subconscious; it had been used at the grammar school, when he was a well-scrubbed scholar there, to describe the hypothetical collision of an irresistible force with an immovable object. Harold Dartie was an immovable object; Dan had to constitute himself an irresistible force. But in pursuit of this purpose, the intervening paradoxes remained. Dan had to be present but absent, mobile but static, voluble but silent; he had to face Harold Dartie without going anywhere near him; he had to be a reliable eyewitness of the murder without having gone anywhere near it.

He needed a large, complex and foolproof plan, and he

needed it immediately. If it was a plan of unimaginable brilliance, he could achieve, or at least attempt, the blankly impossible; if not, he was done for in any one of a dozen possible ways, the most probable being a death at the hands of Harold Dartie, so slow that before it was reached, he would have pointed out the rabbit hole that held the silver.

This depressing thought caused him to go so slowly once again he nearly fell off. He recovered himself; he saw, with the minimum of surprise, a bright cock yellowhammer perched on top of the thorn hedge into which he had nearly collapsed. Another one began to sing, a few yards along the hedge. He was also a gentleman, but not as sulfurous as the first. This one had long stopped breeding; he was changing his clothes into the drabber garments of winter. But he was still singing, and would be for a few weeks yet—still piping monotonously for his little bit of bread and no cheese. The first bird, the brighter bird, suddenly attacked the singer, flying at him along the top of the hedge with a whirring confusion of wings. The singer departed, with an air that said he was not being chased away, but had suddenly remembered an appointment. The aggressive bird returned to his post.

Dan was surprised. He knew yellowhammers laid their first eggs in late April; it was impossible not to know, because they made such a fuss when you went anywhere near a nest. They generally reared a second brood. But this bird was busy with a third, at a time when he'd normally be joining his friends in one of their big autumn flocks. Maybe his second brood had been eaten by a rat or trodden on by somebody clearing the ditches. Dan stood very still, watching. His mother's tea could wait a bit. The bird must be rearing, since he was wearing that brilliant yellow on head and breast, since he was driving away trespassers.

Sure enough the bird dropped off the hedge into the bank below, and scuttled under the thorn twigs. Dan put his bicycle down, crept closer, and ventured a peep. He was care-

ful to disturb the hedge as little as possible, in case a preda-
tor saw the disturbance and profited by it. And there was
the nest, on the bank and well in under the hedge: not one of
the best constructed, but not bad—a roughish cup of dry
grass and moss, lined with hair that had probably come from
beef bullocks who had rubbed it off onto barbed wire. There
were four eggs, about the usual number. They were mau-
vish-white and covered with squiggles that might have been
made by a mad Chinese calligrapher, who had black and
brown and a little red ink, and who used a very fine pen and
a coarse brush. Dan's father had called these birds "writing
larks." He had always used the old names for everything—
indeed Dan suspected that he sometimes invented new old
names (as Dan often did himself, when he was being a professional leprechaun)—but not in this case. Dan's grandfather had gone one further, and called them "scribbling
larks." But he believed, or said he believed, that the writing
meant something: it meant "Don't take my eggs." Dan was
inclined to believe his grandfather. At any rate he obeyed
the message, crept from the place, and wished the birds luck
with their autumn children.

He bicycled slowly away. It was a great deal more pleasant to make the acquaintance of scribbling larks than to con-
template doing battle with Mr Harold Dartie.

It was nearer to birds than battles, coming home and getting his mother's tea. But there was a bit of warfare in the
atmosphere. She was cross because he was late. This was not
because she was hungry. He only wished she could sometimes be hungry. It was because she wanted order, decency,
respectability, in the crazy patchwork of their lives. She
wanted a middle-class routine, and Dan coming home to the
nice little villa and the nice little wife, the one surrounded
by golden privet and the other by dainty things. . . . Her tea
being late made her brood, and brooding on his treachery
made her angry.

39

"Ye ben wenchen or boozen," she stated flatly, not asking a question but delivering judgement. "Ye never ben worken, this hour. What ye do bent work, any road. What's thicky muck on me plate?"

"Wishful thinken," said Dan. "A-bent set a morsel on 'at plate."

He did not as a rule at home talk as broad as this. He did not, of course, use the voice at the other extreme, the clipped banker's voice which could be made to sound, on demand, like a solicitor or even a captain of marines: that would have been rubbing salt into the ever-open wound. But a broad voice made a point. It reminded his mother that he was as obstinate as she was.

She frowned at her plate.

"Yestiddy's mustard," she said, scratching at the plate with a fingernail. "Ben bes' t'bide in a pigsty an' be done. Folk 'd be cleaner."

Dan smiled, and gave her another plate. She looked away from him sharply. It was no good him thinking he could get round her, as though she was one of those brazen modern baggages in the village, by standing there smiling like a gander. She inspected her new plate with a suspicious frown.

She had seen the smile before she turned away. She knew exactly what effect it had on girls, because his father had had the same smile, which had had the same effect, on herself most of all.

As to the plate, she admitted defeat. It was halfway clean. But she would never, never, as long as her eye was sharp and her tongue as sharp as her eye, admit defeat on the larger issue. She'd get him back in that bank before she was done. It was all she had to live for now, and she was by no means ready to die until she'd done it.

Try as he might, Dan got very little food down her, for all she'd been so impatient. It was no good nagging. It was no good her nagging him, either, but that didn't stop her doing it.

*   *   *

40

Dan cleared away and washed up. He heard his mother sniff. It was an unspoken—an almost spoken—criticism of his method of washing up.

It was still broad daylight. Dan felt restless, directionless and frightened. He decided to go out. He had no particular errand. He could think better out of doors than in, and with the company of birds and circling insects rather than the company of his mother.

Seeing him take his old tweed cap from the hook, she said, "Wenchen, boozen or thieven." She used the same flat tone of certainty. She merely added a third activity, of which she assumed he would shortly be guilty, to the two of which she assumed he had been guilty: an evening delinquency to add to those of working hours.

Usually she would have been right.

"Be back in time t'help you t'bed, old lady," said Dan.

She made a noise between a cough and a grunt, expressing every possible hostile and incredulous answer.

Dan never went for walks, as do people who are in the countryside but not of it. He never set a foot to the ground, in any direction, without an objective. This evening stroll was a break with precedent, a first-timer. He was going for a walk.

He was out of the house and loping along the hazardous lane which led to it when he remembered, with astonishment, that he did have an objective. It was a matter he had forgotten all about, in the imminence of Harold Dartie.

His objective was the American girl at the Priory, the performing artist who was about to spend a fortnight washing up and being artistically enriched. The neat-figured, neat-featured little dark girl who had hauled those big cases so easily out of the car. The one who represented for him the charm or challenge of the utterly unfamiliar.

He turned about, and plunged into the Priory Woods. It was a delicate plunge, a medal-winning dive: very little was disturbed, and there was no sound.

There was no sound as he went past the rabbit holes that

41

contained his bank accounts and his silver vaults, except that of the unworried birds in the leaf canopy above him. Only one blackbird, fossicking among fallen leaves, shot away with its needless and hysterical cry of alarm.

Sukie Bush was already regretting it. Her Aunt Helen had brought her to Europe as a post-graduation treat, and Aunt Helen had enrolled both of them in this crazy teach-in.

They had done Rome, Florence, Venice, Avignon, Chartres, Paris, London. Their tour, designed in New York but starting from Miami, had left a series of flashbulb stills on Sukie's mental retina: not so much Michelangelo's David as the shellfish that almost made Aunt Helen throw up; not so much St. Peter's as a greasy, conceited ass-pincher on the Via Veneto; not so much the Palace of the Popes . . . and so forth. It was all far, far too quick. It was a parody of the American cultural zap-zap, European civilisation on a quick-lunch counter, one hour in a city and it's done, its history and its beauties sucked dry, so back into the air-conditioned bus and on, and on, and on. Aunt Helen had loudly despised the whole thing, which was silly, as it was all her idea. Sukie had quite enjoyed it. It did not (except on the Via Veneto) mar her enjoyment that she was much and noisily admired wherever they went. She was used to admiration on campus and at home in Tampa. She had thought that maybe European men had different ideas; it was clear they did not; wolf whistles came out the same in any language, and so did the kind of propositions she had been turning down (not quite invariably) since her junior year in high school. It was not only that. She had enjoyed the strange food, strange sounds, strange smells.

It was a relief to get to a country where they spoke more or less the same language, weird as they made it sound.

And now she was homesick.

But they had met these guys, fellow Americans, in the Cumberland Hotel in London. They were bumming around Europe indefinitely because Deac didn't want to follow his

42

father into the manufacture of toilet paper, and Chuck didn't want to live with his fifth stepfather. They were bumming comfortably and creatively. One thing they had was money. The other thing they had was an Imaginary Circus, the idea presumably stolen from Victoria Chaplin and her French husband. What they did, under a very little "big top," was to mime the whole routine of a regular circus. Animals, clowns, ringmaster, acrobats, tightrope walkers, trapeze artists, everything. To Aunt Helen this sounded fascinating. To Sukie it sounded something that could be interesting for a maximum of five minutes. They had not actually yet performed in public. They were pretty nearly ready to. They had seen advertised this Symposium of the Performing Arts, and it hit them that this was the environment in which they could try their stuff on a sophisticated audience, perfect it, get the timing right, cut any items that didn't go over, and at the same time learn from the other performing artists. They were pretty serious about all this. They must have been, to talk about it for so many hours.

As it happened, Sukie and Aunt Helen were both performing artists. Sukie had majored in drama at college, and she knew all about thinking herself into the essential awareness of an orange crate, or a fish hook, or a church tower. Though she had long ago decided to be not an actress but a dramatic critic, on the long, long road to her degree she had acquired numerous performing skills. Aunt Helen was an interpretive dancer in the school of Isadora Duncan. She had never danced professionally, but she had performed in public, if you counted private parties as public. She wanted to enrich the range and depth of her interpretations. As soon as she heard about the Symposium she was agog. It was the kind of thing she liked. It was pretty cheap. It would do them no harm to live simply, after all that rich food and racketing around. Sukie wanted to go home; but she was at Aunt Helen's financial mercy, so she went to the Symposium instead.

Aunt Helen hired a Hertz through American Express.

43

They offered a ride to Deac and Chuck, but the boys said they wanted a car of their own when they got there.

Aunt Helen was joyful at the prospect not only of enriching her interpretive dancing (and enriching the art of others by it) but also of dwelling for two weeks in the English countryside, of which she had read so often though never seen.

Sukie had seen too much European countryside through the tinted windows of the bus. She wanted to be fishing on her friends' boats, and swimming and playing tennis; she wanted to get started on a career that would eventually make her the distinctive, authoritative voice of American dramatic criticism. Her heart sank as they drove west. Some of the fields were green and had cows on them; some were yellow and had combines on them. Big deal.

They knew the place was a school and also a priory. When they turned a corner of the drive and rolled towards it, Sukie thought they had come to the wrong place. She had seen plenty of schools, and this wasn't like them. She had seen plenty of priories (too many, in Italy), and this wasn't like them. It was like a mental hospital in Salem, Massachusetts, which she had seen in a late-night horror movie.

Around were woods and fields and some tennis courts. There was a small pool which, even from a distance, shone bright green with algae.

They signed some things, the essence of which was that the directorate was not responsible if they fell downstairs and broke a leg.

Deac and Chuck appeared. There was a reunion of a warmth not really justified by their brief London acquaintance. But the boys carried their grips upstairs, up a terrible number of stairs to an airy little room with a lot of little beds in it. Deac showed them the bathroom, which was a mile away. Deac was the one with a blond beard and a denim jacket, about twenty-six, from New York, Columbia graduate, classical jazz buff, etc. Chuck showed them the john,

44

which was another mile away in another direction. He was the one with the black bandito moustache and dirty white T-shirt, a little older, from some other city, dropout from Northwestern, thirties-movie buff, etc.

It was evident at supper that the three of them were by twenty years the youngest people there, except a couple of the staff, who were not artists and would not perform. The sexes were about even, although there were cases that looked marginal to Sukie.

Another thing evident at supper was that the food was terrible.

Yet another was that the people were, if not terrible, at least not good. They all sat on benches at long tables covered in oilcloth, using heavy white plates and very light knives and forks of grey metal. Everybody was placed among strangers, to break the ice. Sukie was between a teacher from Bedfordshire who made and manipulated life-size puppets, and a North London librarian who wrote and sang modern folk songs. They were the same man. At least they were both in their fifties, thin-haired, bespectacled, readers of something called the *Guardian*, liberal voters; they had the painfully refined yap-yap voices that Sukie had heard in British movies and in *Brideshead Revisited* on television, though not at the Cumberland Hotel; they talked across her about themselves.

Three people had not turned up. All had sent apologies and explanations; all had forfeited their substantial deposits. Two were women, sisters, who were said to do something called historical-philosophical duologues. The third was a Mr Justin Squires. Nobody knew what he did. Sukie felt a wave of relief at being spared the duologues, and she thought she was probably right to be relieved at being spared whatever Mr Justin Squires did. A man with a name like that was going to play a medieval one-string fiddle, or sing doleful ballads in Punjabi.

Deac and Chuck asked Sukie to come to the village pub

45

with them. She wavered, close to accepting; she had never seen the inside of an English pub except in photographs in travel ads. Aunt Helen forbade it. She was not against pubs, and certainly not against these cultured and adventurous young men, but she needed Sukie's help to finish unpacking.

Aunt Helen's reaction to the performing artists was quite different. She was already feeling enriched, even after that terrible supper. The people here were very, very different from the group on the bus. (This was certainly true.) Her unpacking finished, she joined a group in a comfortable, shabby room called the common room. It was the only place in the building where smoking was permitted; but there were few smokers. The group included the spindly director of the Symposium, a Mr Marcus Bird, a man of incandescent enthusiasms, as well as the Bedfordshire schoolmaster who made puppets, and other enriching souls. Sukie saw that Aunt Helen was as happy as a lark, and would be sitting there talking for hours.

Sukie went to the school library, which they had been urged to use, but to use with respect. She chose, dubiously but with respect, *The Wind in the Willows*, which as far as she could see was the only readable item on any of the shelves. She settled into a little hard chair to meet the Mole and the Rat again; she felt for the moment too tired and dispirited to face all those stairs. It was a quarter to eleven.

The door opened with a bang, and Deac came in. He staggered a little and he was sweating. He smelled of beer, so much so that he must have spilled a lot on his clothes as well as drunk a lot. From campus experience, Sukie thought it likely that he would throw up; with beer, enough to make you drunk was an awful lot of fluid. Sukie did not want to be present when Deac threw up.

"Ah," said Deac. "Bonanza! The luck of the Irish! Let'sh shtart as we mean to go on, baby." His speech was hoarse but only a little slurred.

He began walking very carefully towards her, using when they came to hand the backs of chairs to support himself.

46

Sukie dropped her book and ran round to the far side of the table where she had been sitting. She looked at Deac crossly. He made it to the other side of the table and stood leaning on it. They stared at one another across two yards of scratched tabletop.

"Be sweet," said Deac. "Act as lovely as you look. We got to perform, you and me. We got to get our act together. Art. *Arsh amatoria.* The ballet of bed. That'sh why we're here, ishn't it?"

"What?" said Sukie, completely surprised.

"Christ, I thought you dug. Sure you dig. Why d'you think I hooked Aunt Whosis on this crummy shym—shympo—"

He lunged round the table, trying to take Sukie by surprise. Without any difficulty she kept the table between them.

"Quit teasing!" shouted Deac.

"But you're a gay," said Sukie, who had simply assumed this at their first meeting.

"I am not! Never wash. It's a lie. Who told you that? Chuck tell you that? It'sh a damned lie. He's the gay. Always was. Not me, baby. Try me. C'mon, try me!"

He somehow scrambled onto the table, and started crossing it towards her on his hands and knees. Sukie ran out of the room and slammed the door behind her. Seeing there was a key in the lock, she locked it. Since the room was on the ground floor, the windowsills not six feet from the ground, Deac was scarcely a prisoner. But he would be delayed for a while.

Safety lay in numbers. Sukie started back to the common room, wishing she had brought *The Wind in the Willows.*

Rounding a corner in the ill-lit passage, she ran into a T-shirt which was sodden with spilled beer. She found she was enfolded in hairy arms, and listening to slurred endearments. That Deac was a fag, but Chuck was a red-blooded man. He'd show her. That was why they were here, wasn't it? She was aware of wet lips and a prickly moustache, on

47

her brow but coming down. She tried to break free. He held her. She was a small girl and he was a big man. She hit him as hard as she could in the solar plexus. She knew about a knee to the groin, but things had not gone far enough for such extreme measures. The punch served. He grunted and let go of her. He began to retch. She ran to the common room.

None of the others looked up when she came in.

She thought about an immediate complaint to the director, in front of the others. She decided on a private complaint in the morning. It had all happened to her before, and it was silly to make a great drama out of it; but if it kept happening it would get to be a terrible bore and it could get to be scary. The two weeks would be dire enough without lecherous drunks.

It was no good talking to Aunt Helen. Aunt Helen would just be envious. Nobody had ever been allowed to try it with Aunt Helen, and so she left it too late, and now they never would.

"Hullo, there, Sukie. Come in and park yourself."

"Thanks, uh, Marcus."

Absolute informality was one of the few rules of the Symposium. You couldn't cross-pollinate when you were calling somebody "Mister."

Sukie said she was not making a complaint, exactly, but she'd like some kind of assurance that it wasn't going to happen every single evening.

"Oh, my poor child," said Marcus Bird, his whole spindly body wriggling with concern. "Oh, my poor precious."

He jumped up from his desk and came round to her chair. He put an arm around her shoulders, and with his other hand tipped up her chin.

"Old Marcus will look after you, sweetie. You're always safe here. No interruptions—"

"Oh, God," said Sukie, and got out of there quick.

* * *

48

Sukie went out onto the lawn, where a spirit of aimlessness prevailed. It was only the first full day; they were all beginners; none of the directing staff had ever run a symposium before, and none of the members had ever attended one. Nobody quite knew what to do, except Francis Mordaunt, the Guildford schoolmaster, who was doing conjuring tricks. That was what he did. He brought eggs out of people's ears. He did it with an air of relaxed indifference, as though he was simply amusing himself and did not want an audience. In fact, Sukie thought, he wanted an audience very badly, all the time. He was a good conjurer, though. Sukie thought he could have been a professional, but she heard him explaining to her Aunt Helen, in a fluting voice higher than Aunt Helen's, that he had a commitment to teaching.

"I do not instruct, I compost young brains to stimulate growth," he cried.

He wanted his own brain to be composted by the Symposium, to widen and deepen the range of his magic. He looked like a middle-aged choirboy, except for his prison uniform of blue cotton. He was better when he was conjuring than when he was talking. He stopped conjuring all too soon, and resumed talking. So Sukie strolled away, alert to evade Deac, Chuck, or Marcus Bird.

They all spent the rest of the day deciding how to spend the next two weeks. It had not been possible to draw up a program until they all knew what talent was available. They'd finish with a full-scale production, everybody contributing, so that they could tell how much they'd all been enriched.

Sukie, challenged about her contribution, said that she had come specifically to get a sense of artistic direction. She'd make a contribution, all right, but she couldn't yet say what it would be. This gritty honesty was much admired.

It was the most boring day Sukie had ever spent.

Deac, Chuck and Marcus Bird all looked at her, whenever

49

they got the chance, with leering complicity. None of them believed her "no." She was being a deliberate tease. She didn't want to seem like too much of a pushover, too much of a tramp, not right away. She needed just a little more working on. That was how their minds were working, the creepy Limey as macho as the Americans. She foresaw needing a blackjack or a pair of brass knuckles. It was still no good talking to Aunt Helen.

After supper—distinctly better than the first night's—she went for a stroll in the grounds. Other people were doing it too, but in groups. She had had enough of groups. There were hints here and there that performing artists were spreading their wings, tentatively, to their new friends. Sukie heard some kind of folk song, and some kind of dialect recitation; and Aunt Helen in the distance was showing a tendency to swoop to and fro in an interpretive way.

Grumpily, safe from everybody for a while, Sukie walked along the edge of a wood two hundred yards from the house.

"The sweet o' the evenen t'ye, liddle missie," said a voice like the slow pouring of maple syrup onto a waffle, not like any voice Sukie had ever heard.

A face followed the voice. It was not quite like any face Sukie had ever seen—smooth as a child's, yet deeply weatherbeaten, wedge-shaped, with untidy mousy hair, and with eyes of an astonishing cornflower blue.

It was a little man, in rough country clothes. Sukie supposed he worked around the place. His voice was a peasant's, but his face was not quite a peasant's. He was strange, like an elf, like something in a fairy tale.

The strange little man grinned at her. There was no mistaking the admiration in his grin. There was no mistaking the lechery in it.

"Oh, God," said Sukie in sudden fury. "Even the help are as horny as tomcats."

4

DAN WAS NONPLUSSED. "Even the help are as horny as tomcats" was not a phrase he could immediately translate, but from the tone in which the girl said it, and the expression on her face, it was obviously hostile.

He had arrived a few minutes before, and seen people coming out of the Priory onto the gravel and the lawns. The girl was not among them. Surely she would be, on such an evening. The people strolling and talking were enjoying themselves. There were bursts of laughter. To Dan the whole scene was more civilised, more congenial, than he had expected. If the conversations the people were having were actually dull, this was unimportant, because the people who were having them thought they were fascinating.

Dan was pleased to see the little dark girl finally coming out into the golden evening. Her hands were deep in the pockets of her pants. She didn't join any of the groups and she wasn't going to. She was like someone in a cartoon strip, going along under a dark cloud. Dan hoped he might cheer her up. He positioned himself in the edge of the wood so as to intercept her. As she neared him, he saw that she was even more attractive than he had dared hope—a miniature

51

beauty with a broad brow, a little pointed nose, a little pointed chin, wide-set grey eyes, a hint of freckles, a perfect figure.

His opening gambit was his normal one. It did not have the normal effect. The comic-yokel voice, the softening-up smile, were an unqualified failure. He tried an entirely different approach.

"I beg your pardon," he said in his banker's voice, his blue-suit and little-black-shoes voice. "I live locally, you know. I was interested to observe performing artists. We get very few of them down here."

She looked at him wide-eyed. Hostility had not been replaced by amazement in her face, but joined by it.

Dan kept his own face serious and respectful. It was not an expression natural to him when he was talking to a beautiful girl, but it seemed to enrage her less than his smile did.

He said, "May I ask in what capacity you perform?"

She said, frowning, "Do you work here?"

"No. Simply taking the evening air, like yourself. Impelled here by curiosity."

He had been impelled there by her; to most girls he would have said so; the time for that might come, but it had not come yet.

"Why are you hiding in the woods?" she asked.

"Bashfulness," said Dan. "The shrinking violet. I'm one of the things you see when you move an old log."

"Why did you start talking in that weird voice?"

"Strangers usually like it. Echo of our heritage. Putting it another way, I'm a professional relic of the rural past."

"It's just a fraud?"

"Oils the wheels of commerce," said Dan, "while providing innocent merriment."

Much of the hostility had disappeared from the girl's face. She looked better with an expression of curiosity. Dan liked her close-cropped dark hair; he liked all that he could see of her and all that he could guess at.

52

He risked his broadest voice again, since it seemed to intrigue her: "They Lunnon folk ben girt struck, seemenly, wi' me olden words an' sich."

"Now I can't understand a word you're saying."

"Oh, it's not meant to be understood," said Dan in his banker's voice. "Just background music."

"You ought to join this crazy party. And perform that voice."

"Hum," said Dan, possibilities opening up in front of him like the doors of a thousand beach huts.

What Sukie saw, after the first few seconds, was a man she didn't have to be afraid of. He couldn't push her around. He was too small, too frail, too bashful after she had batted down his opening freshness. He was a fraud, putting on that crazy incomprehensible act, and therefore vulnerable to exposure.

Sukie was stuck here in this priory for two weeks, because Aunt Helen was in love with the whole deal. She needed a bodyguard. She needed to be visibly escorted, to neutralise Deac and Chuck and the wet-palmed Marcus Bird. Bodyguards could take over, but not this character. He was gentle. He was cute, but a kind of nothing. He was old, over thirty, at least ten years older than herself. It would be convenient to have him around. It would make the Priory tolerable. He was risk-free insurance.

Sukie was not accustomed to using or manipulating people, but this seemed a good moment to begin.

She said, "Your name is Justin Squires. You talk with that British yap, if you know what I mean, but your act is that other voice. You enrolled in this thing, and you paid the deposit, but you sent a message you couldn't come. Now after all here you are."

The little man looked at her in silence for a moment, half in and half out of the bushes he was occupying. He did have amazing blue eyes. They were just blue eyes. Sukie had friends of Swedish and Swiss ancestry with similar eyes, and one friend, with the most brilliant blue eyes of all, who was a Polish Jew. She was not about to go weak at the knees because somebody's eyes were one colour rather than another.

"Hum," he said. "I'll be unmasked within ten seconds and thrown out within twenty."

"Chicken."

"Somebody must know this—what?—did you say Justin Squires?"

"Nobody here ever saw him. Nobody knows anything about him."

"I can't live up to a name like that."

"It's just the name the guy has."

"Surely not. He invented it."

Sukie found herself pleading with the little brown man, cajoling him, pressing him to impersonate Mr Justin Squires for an aesthetic and ascetic two weeks at Medwell Priory. In the course of this effort she found herself smiling. She felt dishonest, smiling at a person she was planning to use simply as security, simply as cover, simply in order to get a quiet life.

She despised herself for the smile; but it seemed the smile worked. His own answering smile was brief and bashful; he said, reluctantly, that he would pack a few things and turn up later in the evening.

He made a gesture of farewell, smiled shyly, and disappeared into the woods from which he had only half emerged.

Sukie felt a sense of power. She would have to have been very dumb, which she was not, not to be aware that a lot of men found her attractive, and that she could often get her own way as a result. But to persuade a total stranger, with a few minutes' conversation and one smile, to do something so crazy, something criminal even . . . Maybe European food had done mysterious things to her; maybe that little creature of the woods never got to see any pretty girls.

It really was, for her, a beautiful solution to problems that had seemed more than she could bear. An appeal to Deac for protection against Chuck and Marcus Bird would have seemed, to Deac, like the most blatant invitation. And the other way about. Her appeal to Marcus Bird *had* seemed a blatant invitation. Now they were all checkmated. She had somebody riding shotgun. Obviously Deac or Chuck could pick "Justin Squires" up between finger and thumb and remove him out of the way; but she thought neither would resort to crude violence.

It occurred to her some minutes later that "Justin Squires" had a funny way of life if he could suddenly drop out of it for two weeks. What did he do? What was he? Where did he really come from?

Some minutes after that it occurred to her that her own attitude must have seemed pretty peculiar. Why should she suddenly be so anxious that he should drop everything and join the Symposium? She had not attempted any explanation of this, and he had not asked for any. Could he think she'd fallen for him? What else *could* he think? Was she in worse trouble, four tomcats instead of three? No—one thing she was very sure of was that she could handle the little man. Anybody who had survived four years on her campus, and the ass-pinchers of the Via Veneto, could deal with somebody whose whole stock-in-trade seemed to be blue eyes and a phony maple-syrup voice.

As a performing artist, that voice probably put him on a level with most of the others. Could he handle conversations with the Bedfordshire teacher and the London librarian? Probably not. That was not terribly important. Sukie herself had hardly attempted to talk to them or to anybody else.

Dan walked home thoroughly pleased and thoroughly puzzled.

The idea of actually joining the Symposium had simply never occurred to him. But it was, in many ways, a marvellous solution to his most immediate problems. He was as close at hand as though he were at home. He could keep an eye on his mother and on the dogs and birds. He could use a telephone—some telephone, somewhere in the Priory—to reassure the nobs who would be expecting him to come and be a pixie in their gardens. Yet he would be completely out of sight of the village and of Mr Harold Dartie; swallowed up by those intense, self-conscious people, wrapped around by them as though by an invisible cloak. Nobody local was going near the place, and the new school caretakers didn't know Dan by sight. He could go into the village, if he had to, in his own time and in his own way; he could go to Medwell Court, equally privately, if that seemed a good idea.

He had given himself a bit of time to do something about Mr Harold Dartie. A fortnight. What he was going to do he had not the slightest idea; but he had fourteen days and nights in which to get an idea.

That was one puzzle. The other was the girl. The change in the girl. One minute snapping at him in evident fury and contempt, the next smiling and making this preposterous, this God-sent suggestion. Why? Dan had had many successes with many girls, but he did not believe in the instant adoration of a girl like that. She was very pretty and she must know it. Her face had a provocative quality, and her smile was broad and sweet. She must know about that, and about her figure and the way she moved. She wouldn't be exactly desperate for admiration or company. It was rum.

"Justin Squires," he thought. He tried and completely failed to picture the owner of such a name. Of all the names he had ever heard, or invented, it seemed to fit himself least.

He could say he worked in a bank. It seemed they were people like that, not professional performers. He thought he could remember enough about the hated days of his peonage to make the bank story credible. If there was a real banker at the Priory, he would simply refuse to talk shop. "I came here to get away from all that." Yes, that rang true enough.

56

Where did he come from? West Mugton. It had the merit, as a place of origin, of not existing. How was he getting to the Priory? A lift from the station, in the car of a kindly stranger, then a short walk. Why had he changed his plans, and then changed them back again? Holiday unexpectedly cancelled owing to illness of manager. Manager cured, false alarm, wrong diagnosis, Mr Squires at liberty after all. No problems there.

Performing? That was another problem for another day. The girl seemed to think he'd get by. He felt a little bashful about it. What the girl did he never had discovered. He didn't know her name, either, or she his. He knew nothing in the world about her except that she came from America. Their relationship had got off to a most eccentric start.

Dan's mother said it was time for her bed, and the dogs said it was time for a run, and Gloria, tamest and most confiding of the blue-marble bantams, fluttered up to his shoulder and whispered in his ear that it was time for another scoop of corn. He had a complicated half hour.

When his mother was in bed and peace out of doors restored, he got out his respectable suitcase, once the property of Sir George Simpson. In it he put his respectable clothes. He had nothing resembling the prison-uniform blue denim favoured by the male members of the Symposium; but he thought anybody called Justin Squires would have an individual style of dress. He packed what he had and hoped for the best.

He did not let his mother see his dark banker's suit before he packed it. The sight of it turned knives in wounds.

For his actual arrival at the Priory—by an irony that gave him no pleasure—Dan was dressed almost exactly as he had been for his arrival at Medwell Court two nights previously. He did not, however, have his cap, screwdriver or weighted blackthorn. Instead he had fifty pounds in used fivers, from

57

the rabbit hole which was his current account, as an instalment on the price of the Symposium, which the American girl had said would be required.

He arrived with his suitcase just as full darkness fell. There were still people strolling outside; Dan imaged they were being bitten by bugs and bombed by moths.

A girl with spectacles answered his ring at the front door. He recognised her as one of the staff. She was much unlike the American girl. Behind her in the enormous hall, under a large and hideous electric chandelier, were a dozen people. Dan faced them all in sudden bashfulness. He was pleased to see the American girl among them.

"I scratched my entry," said Dan.

The girl in glasses looked at him blankly. He realised that he had chosen the wrong words. They were the words of a captain of marines, not those of a performing artist–assistant bank manager.

He cleared his throat and started again: "I was obliged to notify you of my inability to attend," he said, as though dictating a business letter at a big desk. "But circumstances have in the event permitted my arrival."

"Oh, yes," said the girl. "That's fine. You are . . . ?"

Dan had a moment of paralysing blankness. Who was he? That name was ridiculous and it had gone clean out of his head. This was the immediate and humiliating end of the adventure.

"You must be Mr Squires," said the American girl, suddenly and very loudly.

"Justin Squires," said Dan thankfully. "I hope I may, ah, re-enlist in the group."

He might, indeed. He was presented to all those present, whose names confused him. They all seemed to be names like his new name. The name most like his of all of them he did catch: Marcus Bird, director of the Symposium. He got Sukie Bush as well. He was glad to know that one.

He was led away to sign a paper. This alarmed him.

58

Somebody only had to compare this signature with a previous signature, which they must have ... but people didn't spend their time sitting about and comparing signatures. Dan thought the risk was real but small. It had to be run. He signed boldly. He paid his fifty pounds. They were surprised to be paid in cash, but not at all displeased.

He was shown to an upstairs dormitory in which, as it happened, he had once hidden from the police and the whole local population. He was sharing it with three others. He expected in time to be able to tell them apart and to remember their names.

He was heartily addressed as Justin immediately, by everybody, when he went downstairs and found the common room, where people were.

He said his performing art was the re-creation of a vanished peasant culture. He had the impression, though nobody came right out and said it, that this was generally regarded as a pretty dim and unadventurous activity: it was not to be compared with life-size puppets or interpretive dancing.

"I think it will be very, very enriching," said the girl called Sukie Bush. Dan thought she was joking, but he was far from sure. American girls, judged by this sample, were unpredictable and impossible to understand.

Two other young Americans, but not so young and not nearly so pretty, came in a little drunk. They had been to the Chestnut Horse. They had been hearing details of the sensational local murder; they had even been meeting the new owner of the stately home where the murder had been committed. Their account of it was garbled.

As soon as they came in, Sukie Bush crossed the room to the corner where Dan was working at being invisible. She began telling him about her tour of Europe with her Aunt Helen.

There was a pleasant ceremony called the Nightcap, at this moment inaugurated at somebody's suggestion; it involved a tray of mugs and a boiling kettle. On offer were tea, instant coffee, Bovril and Knorr bouillon cubes. There was a general raising of mugs and calling of toasts.

"Is Sukie really Susan?" Dan asked the girl, in a break in her account of Paris.

"No. Sukie Mae is the name I was given. I dropped the Mae. My mother still uses the whole thing, and Aunt Helen when she's mad at me."

Dan felt out of his depth. But he had been accepted into the Symposium. His double life had begun.

Dan that night pretended to snore, a thing he had never done. His roommates thought they were waking him. He feigned immediate sleep and renewed snoring.

As he expected, he was asked in the morning to move into another dormitory by himself. He did so with apparent reluctance.

Sukie and her aunt were on the floor above, with all the rest of the women. Much traffic between the floors was improbable, owing to the average age of the Symposium. Some was obviously possible. Dan had no idea if he would be joining it.

He had no idea how to deal with his other and larger problems.

During his first full day as a member of the Symposium, Dan found that he could come and go as he pleased. He was so inconspicuous that his absence was no more noticed than his presence. There were plenty of dominant personalities, the automatic centres of groups—Sukie's Aunt Helen, the American young men who imitated elephants and acrobats, Robin Callender-Smith, the Bedfordshire schoolmaster, with his life-size puppets—and the groups they were centres of had silent fringes. Dan could leave or join these fringes without comment. Therefore he could slip away to feed his mother and his menagerie, and come back to find performing artists enriching one another.

60

His mother knew he was up to some mischief. She disdained to ask him about it. She would, if it came to the point, be unswervingly loyal. Her technique if anybody came asking questions was to become deaf-mute and mad. That was her performance; she enjoyed it, but not if she was required to go on doing it for too long.

Dan was startled by the public warmth of Sukie Bush's greeting when he rejoined his fellow artists after putting his mother to bed. It was as though she was performing: as though her act was representing a young female who had one friend more loved and trusted than anybody else in the world.

It all grew no less rum.

The big young Americans who imitated a circus looked at him, he thought, a little sourly. But as, by this time of night, they were back from the Chestnut Horse, there might be many reasons for that.

With the ceremony of the Nightcap there was a song recital. The North London librarian, allegedly called Jeremy Chalice, had during the day composed, and now performed, a modern folk song about the Symposium:

> I rode a rail to the West Countree
> Performing artists for to see . . .

There was a chorus, in which all present were supposed to join. The quality and variety of the voices were at first astonishing, but then were dominated, as soon as she had mastered the words and tune of the chorus, by Sukie's Aunt Helen:

> Montparnasse of the West Countree
> Is Med-Med-Medwell Prioree!

There was happy and prolonged laughter after the song, and applause of that special warmth which people reserve for group performances in which they have taken part.

61

Sukie, sitting with Dan in a corner of the common room, did not join in the song. Dan was therefore bashful about doing so, although he had enjoyed the simple little song.

Dan borrowed the telephone in what was usually the headmistress's study. He telephoned to Sir George Simpson, Mr Edwin Calloway and others. He used a voice so antique and treacly that he wondered if it would travel down the wires. He said he would not be mowing their lawns or mending their sheds for a fortnight, as he was suffering from "they galloppen gargles." It was a disease none of them would identify, nor Dr Smith diagnose, as he had just invented it. The symptoms, as he described them, were something between hay fever and a severe chill. He said that he was infectious, though he put it in a quainter way, and should not be visited. He did not need the doctor. His mother would look after him, as she had always done. There were such clucks of sympathy and concern on the telephone that he felt an unusual twinge of guilt.

Dan thought it must help—at some future time, and in some unguessable way—to know something about Mr Harold Dartie. Was he in the way of often shooting people in the chest at point-blank range with a big automatic, or did he do it quite rarely? That was the sort of question Dan wanted answered. The usual listening post, the bar of the Chestnut Horse, had not turned up anybody who knew anything about Mr Harold Dartie at all. He had said nothing about his own past, his business, his background, in the pub or anywhere else. If people had asked him, he had avoided answering. Probably very few people had come anywhere near openly asking him about the business from which he had presumably retired: nobody in the village would want to be obviously nosey about the private affairs of this powerful newcomer.

Would the police have investigated his background? Why

would they? Why would they take the trouble? He was the victim, and far away at the time.

Dan realised what he cursed himself for not having realised long before: he had the means to investigate rather fully. He had an address book full of names with which, obviously, Mr Harold Dartie was or had been in contact.

Dan cursed himself again, for not noting down Mr Harold Dartie's previous address and telephone number, and those of his insurance company and the security company he employed. All that information was on the correspondence which he had put back in the briefcase. He should have foreseen that he would want it. He cursed himself less when he reflected that the new owner of Medwell Court being the burglar and murderer was not something he could reasonably have expected.

That evening, in a brief interval in the complexities of looking after his mother and the rest of the family, Dan retrieved the address book from its hiding place.

The following morning he slipped away from a group which was being enriched by Francis Mordaunt's conjuring. He went with regret. He liked conjurers. He went to the telephone in the headmistress's study, and began working through the address book.

He varied his approach according to the strength of accent which answered him, the apparent command of English, the status of the establishment he was calling, as far as that could be guessed from its name and address. He was sometimes a banker, sometimes a solicitor, sometimes an estate agent, asking the restaurants if they were supplied goods or services by Mr Harold Dartie; sometimes he was a gourmet to whom the Shanghai Takeaway had been recommended by his good friend Mr Harold Dartie. He borrowed the names of Robin Callender-Smith, Jeremy Chalice and Francis Mordaunt. Something inhibited him from announcing himself as Justin Squires.

After ninety minutes of telephoning, Dan had tried every

single one of the numbers in the address book. A surprising number—eleven in all—were out of order or unobtainable. Dan tried these via the operator; they had been discontinued, and the numbers not yet reallocated. Dan thought it odd that a restaurant could stay in business without a telephone. Of those who answered, there were some with whom no meaningful communication could take place; the speakers could not understand Dan's questions, nor he their answers. With the majority Dan was able to talk, and much good it did him. Not one single one of them had ever heard of Mr Harold Dartie.

Dan pondered. There must a reason for having all those names and addresses, all typed out and clipped in a ring binder. Obviously there were two major possibilities. One: Harold Dartie did in fact do business with all those funny little eating places, but did it under a different identity, or through an agent; this might be because he had a criminal record or a bad local reputation, or for any of a hundred other reasons, some of which might be perfectly innocent. Two: Harold Dartie had some completely different reason for going about with a kind of specialized gastronomic guide. He might be working for Egon Ronay. He might be proposing to sell them something, quite openly and legally, at some future date.

Dan was inclined to favor the first alternative. Either Mr Harold Dartie did not exist—had, perhaps, been born specifically in order to become squire of Medwell with a new and innocent personality—or somebody else did not exist, who had been doing business with all those diligent Indians and Chinese.

Put it all against what Dan had seen, in the back hall of the Court at two in the morning, and it added up to a devious and sophisticated operator as well as a ruthless killer. A clever spider as well as a greedy one. It looked long odds against the fly.

Dan sighed as he thought of his dogs and his mother and his birds trying to manage without him.

64

*　*　*

By the third or fourth day, a kind of routine democratically established itself, which was exactly the way Marcus Bird said he wanted it to be. The assistant director, Margot Dean—she of the short grey hair, the red trousers, the decisive manner—had an air of wishing the routine were imposed from above, and by her, but the others were having none of that.

After a breakfast marked by a heavy consumption of yogurt and granola, the team whose turn it was cleared away and washed up. Beds were made and rooms swept. Then there was deliberate fragmentation, before the togetherness of lunch. People cross-pollinated in small groups. Sukie's Aunt Helen worked on a dance which interpreted for the very first time the movements and, she said, the emotions of a puppet; she said she was enriched by the experience of Robin Callender-Smith's puppet performances. Robin Callender-Smith did not say if his puppets were enriched by Aunt Helen's dancing. Nobody mentioned *Petroushka* out loud, although Sukie confided to Dan that a dancer being a puppet had been done before, in one of the most celebrated ballets of the twentieth century. Dan nodded as he thought Mr Justin Squires would have nodded.

Lunch developed into a sort of buffet, which spread itself out over the lawn. Dan thought how much his mother would have disapproved of such gypsying.

The afternoon became a time of private practice, meditation and study. Snores could be heard.

Groups coalesced in the early evening, and supermarket wine was poured. Dan missed this phase, loping off through the Priory Woods to look after his household. He was not sorry to miss it, having acquired a taste for better wine. He continued to be startled by the warmth and possessiveness of Sukie's greeting when he rejoined them, and the way she stuck close to him through the rest of the evening. But a sure instinct told him that it did not mean what, with any other girl, it would so obviously have meant. Sukie was still a

65

creature from another planet. He had some value for her which had nothing to do with his blue eyes, his lecherous smile, or any of his voices. Any unequivocal advance would have been rejected, he knew, with rage and contempt. He did not want Sukie's rage and contempt. He wanted her. He despaired of getting her. Meanwhile he greatly enjoyed looking at her and talking to her and being her special friend at the Symposium. The situation was without precedent.

After supper there were a few departures to the Chestnut Horse. Deac and Chuck were the only nightly carousers. The Nightcap ceremony was now always rounded off by the singing of "The Ballad of Medwell Priory," all present, except Sukie and Dan, joining in the inspiriting chorus. And so to a chaste and early bed.

And all the time Dan tried to understand the strange, transatlantic workings of Sukie's mind; and all the time he wondered what to do about Mr Harold Dartie.

News came from the Chestnut Horse, carried more or less ungarbled by Deac and Chuck. The police had found a self-drive hired van in the Milchester Station car park. Bullets in it matched those found in Derek Davis. This suggested, to the collective wisdom of the Chestnut Horse regulars, as quoted by Deac and Chuck, either that the murderer had had an accomplice who had double-crossed him by driving away with the loot, or that another and quite separate villain had happened on the scene, either in the self-drive van or appropriating the murderer's self-drive van, or that the bullets in the van had somehow got there before Derek Davis was killed, or that the murderer had dropped his gun and somebody else had picked it up and shot at him as he was driving away. There had been other suggestions, said the Americans, but these were the ones popularly supported.

The van had been hired by Mr Harold Dartie, to take things he did not want to trust to the removers from his old home to his new one. It had been stolen during the night of the murder from outside his house in Weymouth. He had reported the theft in the morning, the moment he was aware of it. His briefcase had been in the van, which was of course locked. In the briefcase were papers which would have told the villain about the silver, and about the house being empty except for one security man. All this had just come out, in a statement by the Milchester police. Anybody who had seen the van was asked to come forward. The co-operation of the public was earnestly requested; this was the reason for the police statement.

So, Dan thought, the scenario as devised by Mr Harold Dartie was totally convincing. No doubt he had a water-proof phony alibi for that night. Dan felt a wave of despair. He had ten days of safety in the bosom of the Symposium: then what?

Another, minor news item from the pub was that Fred Dawson's van had been found in Weymouth. It might have been driven there by the murderer; it might have been taken by any one of fifty million other people. A funny sort of walking stick had been found in it. This was now the property of Fred Dawson, who was said to be pleased with it.

Nobody had seen Dan's home-made blackthorn with the weight in the handle, because he had only taken it on the kind of expedition when he took trouble not to be seen. At least, he thought it could not be traced to him. He wondered whether, taking a leaf out of Mr Dartie's book, he should re-port its loss to the police. He decided against this.

It was the only decision he felt capable of taking, except to try to find a way to save his life during the next ten days.

5

A LITTLE GUILTILY, Sukie Bush was pleased with herself. She and "Justin Squires" made a couple, an evident and public pairing-off. It was remarked on, indulgently. There were other pairings, of like-minded souls coming sinlessly together. It was noticed that when Justin and Sukie were together, Sukie did all the talking. This was natural, since she had seen so much of the world, if only from the windows of a bus, and he had seen so little of it. She was a future drama critic and he was an assistant bank manager; she just naturally had a lot more to talk about. Meanwhile Deac and Chuck had crossly accepted the situation; so, more reluctantly, had Marcus Bird. The plan had worked and would go on working.

And there was still nothing to be feared from Justin Squires. Alone with him, Sukie was as safe as with Aunt Helen. Sukie almost despised him for being so unthreatening. He wasn't a real man. Not a fag, but not red-blooded. A dominating mother was the reason he was undersexed, Sukie guessed. It was a familiar situation in Tampa; no doubt it happened all over.

She wondered a little about him. But he gave nothing away about himself. When she asked him his real name, he

69

said "Wurzel Gummidge" or "Tom Cobley" or "Will Waterproof." When she asked him what he really did, he said he pretended to do a lot of things, but in truth he didn't do much of anything. When she asked him where he went, when he disappeared each evening, he said he had to report daily to the village policeman, or get an injection from the doctor for his galloping gargles, or feed his boa constrictor. He had not used again to her the broad, rural, incomprehensible accent with which he had first greeted her. He had not used it in public, either, keeping the performance he was ultimately committed to under wraps until the big moment.

He said he was unmarried. She believed him. It figured.

When he slipped away in the evening, he did so imperceptibly. This was possible because he was, so to speak, imperceptible all the time. If people didn't notice him when he was there, except as being her escort, they didn't notice that he wasn't. Sukie thought she was the only one who was aware of his absences, and that was only because she was using him. She had never actually seen him leave. She found she wanted to do so. She found she wanted to follow him, to see where he really went, what he really did. It was not that she was specially curious about him as a person—he hardly existed as a three-dimensional individual—but she had so little to occupy her mind that any little mystery became worth solving. It was like doing a crossword on an airplane. It was not important but it passed the time.

On the seventh evening—simply because she was bored, simply because she wanted to exercise a mind that demanded to be busy and had nothing to busy itself with—Sukie made herself as imperceptible as Justin (a much more difficult thing to do) and kept an eye on him. For the first time she saw the moment of his departure, and the direction of his departure. Had she not been deliberately and closely observing him, she would have missed it. He gave the impression not so much of going on his feet into the woods, as of being silently absorbed by them. She followed him. She

70

managed to keep him in sight, through a tangle of woodland.

She happened to be wearing pretty good camouflage—jeans and a green shirt. She happened to be pretty good at going through a wood quietly, having learned fieldcraft and woodcraft at summer camp when she was in junior high school.

Justin led her to a crazy little Hansel-and-Gretel cottage on the edge of the woods. It seemed to grow out of the woods, to be part of them as a nose is part of a face. Dogs barked excitedly.

Sukie blinked in disbelief. It was not credible that Justin Squires, with his neat English country clothes and his educated yapping English voice, belonged in such a place. He was visiting it. It belonged, maybe, to an old servant of his family.

And there was the servant. An old woman appeared in the open door of the cottage. She was even neater than Justin—neat, and clean, and leaning on a stick, and angry. She went indoors, moving slowly and painfully. Justin followed her, as meekly as he always followed Sukie.

Presently Justin came out. He rattled something in a big can. A lot of small silvery hens with feathery legs came running out of a shed. He threw them the corn he had been rattling in the can. One of the hens fluttered up onto his shoulder; he fed it from the palm of his hand.

Justin let three dogs out of a pen in front of a kennel. They jumped all over him, then ran around. The smallest, a black and white terrier, rushed back to Justin and scrabbled adoringly at his legs. Sukie froze. The gundog among the three—Sukie thought it was a gundog—would scent her, find her, give her away. Sukie did not want to be given away. She was committing no crime, but Justin would be certain to misunderstand. He'd almost be entitled to. He'd think all kinds of things she didn't want him thinking—that she was interested in him, curious about him. Even he might get ideas; even he might make a pest of himself.

71

In fact the dogs were too interested in their suppers to come trailing spies in the woods.

It was obvious that the dogs were his dogs. It was obvious that the hen that flew on his shoulder was his hen. Therefore this was his cottage. And the tidy old woman was not his old servant but his mother, the one whose dominance and possessiveness had turned him, the way Sukie figured it, into the nothing he was.

It was completely weird. It was almost impossible to imagine anybody living in such a place; it was impossible to imagine Justin Squires living in it. Sukie knew she knew very little about England; but she could appreciate the obvious differences between Robin Callender-Smith, say, on the one hand, and George Plummer, the caretaker at the Priory, on the other. Justin supremely obviously inhabited Robin's level rather than George Plummer's, although he entirely lacked the puppeteer's charisma. Robin could in no way be pictured in this gingerbread hovel. So what was Justin doing here?

Although she was missing the Valpollicella which she knew was being poured on the Priory lawn, Sukie stayed crouched in the bushes, looking and listening, completely puzzled. She made certain that she was well hidden and that she made no noise at all.

Dan wondered why Sukie Bush was following him. He had been aware of her doing so before he left the Priory—aware that she was lurking, when she was not given to anything you could call lurking, that she was watching him, which she was not given to, either.

He could easily have given her the slip in the woods, or led her round in a circle and then gone home on his own and at his leisure. He decided that if she wanted to look at his cottage, he would let her. It had not repelled other girls. She could look all she liked at his dogs, his bantams, and his mother. She could not expose him to the rest of the Symposium without exposing herself; if he was an impostor, she had introduced him for reasons which were still utterly mysterious. Perhaps for no reasons. Perhaps American girls were given to picking up strangers and turning them into poodles; perhaps just this American girl was.

Their relationship had not really progressed at all. He knew a great deal about Sukie's European journeys and about life in Florida, but he knew hardly any more about Sukie herself than he had learned on the first evening. Something was needed to jolt them into a new stage; points in the railway had to be changed, to send the train in a better direction. Not, perhaps, the reason why he was burying himself in the Symposium; at least, not yet. Possibly the sight of his dogs would do it, or Gloria the bantam courtesan, who got extra corn by dint of shameless flattery. It was a good idea, perhaps, to remind Sukie that he was not an assistant bank manager with a yappy voice.

She imagined she had crept here silently; she imagined she was now hidden. He supposed she would creep away, with an equal attempt at stealth. And that she would not afterwards say anything to him about it. Was it simple curiosity? Should he be flattered? Or dismayed? Could he now be more relaxed with her, or should he be more on his guard? He had no idea what the girl was about. Until the matter of Mr Harold Dartie was resolved, Sukie's motives were the least of his problems.

Meanwhile she was still useful to him, as being the means by which he was staying alive. And meanwhile she was still a very, very attractive girl. Familiarity had not bred any contempt in Dan for those wide grey eyes, that turned-up nose, those tanned cheeks with the suggestion of freckles, that superb small-scale figure.

He wondered whether to go and talk to her, or to tell the dogs to do so. It was a bad idea. She would be humiliated and angry at being caught snooping. There was no point in hurting her feelings. There was every need to keep her friendship. Dan decided to go on pretending she wasn't there.

73

Dan gave himself a glass of whisky, and drank it in the evening sun outside the cottage. He did not mind her seeing that, either.

When he went back to the Priory for supper, he pretended not to hear her crashing along behind him.

There was more news at Nightcap time from the Chestnut Horse. The new squire of Medwell Court had started moving in his furniture. He was still staying in the pub; Deac and Chuck had had a drink with him. He already seemed to know all the people who came to the pub, the Americans said; he seemed a very popular guy. He bought a few drinks, without being ostentatiously lavish about it. It seemed he had retired, though he was young to have done so. Nobody knew what he had retired from. He was a widower, childless. He liked kids. He was talking about that with Deac and Chuck. When the term started again at the village school, and he was settled into his new home, he was going to have the kids over to the big house in batches. They would have barbecues and all kinds of games. He was fixing it with the head teacher of the school.

Ted Goldingham, the landlord of the Chestnut Horse, had told Deac that Mr Dartie was already a lot more popular in the village than the guy who sold him the Court. You could see why.

Why did a childless widower want a house as big as that? Why, for entertaining, for housing his collections of furniture and paintings and Persian carpets, for putting on functions for charity—he said he really needed the space for doing all the things he promised himself.

The Americans—Deac, Chuck and Sukie's Aunt Helen— were interested in this evidence of the survival of feudal attitudes in the British countryside. They were a little shocked by it. Nobody told them that the attitude of the village was not feudal but commercial. Mr Dartie was not regarded as a lord but as a meal ticket. The village foresaw not leadership but handouts. It would have been cruel to say this to the

74

Americans. It would have been cruel to say it to the Londoners, as well—to Jeremy Chalice and Marcus Bird and the others, to whom the life of Medwell Fratrorum was just as strange as it was to Sukie's Aunt Helen.

There was a good deal of earnest talk about social mobility in the English class structure. Robin Callender-Smith, who taught history at home in Bedfordshire, gave a kind of lecture about it. Elizabethan lawyers, Georgian iron-founders, Victorian bankers and builders, bought themselves the lordships of manors and set up as country squires. Mr Dartie was in this grand tradition. The members of the Symposium who were present listened with respectful attention. They were all learning all the time, as they had been promised in the prospectus.

Dan and Sukie listened too. Dan listened because it was the way to remain an integral, inconspicuous part of the group. At that moment, listening to a lecture on English social history was what you did. Sukie seemed to be interested.

Sukie's attitude to Dan seemed to be quite unchanged by her having seen his cottage, his mother, his dogs, his bantams. She had rejoined the Symposium two minutes after Dan had done so, a twig in her hair from pushing through the Priory Woods. She had treated him with her usual friendly possessiveness. Dan wondered what was going through her lovely little head. He was quite baffled by her. She was as strange to him as the new squire of Medwell was to her Aunt Helen.

On the eighth evening—Saturday, midway point of the Symposium—there was to be a kind of provisional performance by everybody. This had not been part of the original plan, but the general opinion was that it would help them all. Sunday would be spent in discussion about the performances. No one was to mind what was said. Everything would be constructive, helpful; the members of the Symposium knew one another well enough by now to be sure there would be nothing but goodwill in any criticisms. Stronger in

75

their performances, wiser, they would go forward to the following Saturday and to their final performances. It would be highly interesting to see the differences between the two evenings. It was expected that the performers themselves would be keenly aware of differences in themselves and in their work.

Dan was appalled. Performing in private, as to Sir George Simpson, was one thing; the thought of performing in public made his palms sweat and his mouth feel dry. He had given no thought to what he might do, on an improvised stage, in a spotlight, in front of all these clever people. He had had other things to occupy his mind; he had not really believed in the notion of himself getting up and giving a recitation; it had seemed a thing that simply would not happen. But it would happen to Justin Squires. Why else was he here? A recitation, was that what was called for? What recitation? Must he write himself a script? Evidently the others had already done so, and in many cases had done so years before.

Dan confided a little of his horror to Sukie. She looked at him with pitying contempt. After four years studying drama she was well used to footlights, and to a sea of expectant faces dimly seen beyond them. She said there was nothing to be scared of. Nobody was going to shoot him, or burn him at the stake for not being a better performer, or duck him in the grass-green swimming pool for insulting their intelligence. The worst he could do was make a fool of himself, and some of the others were going to do that too. She was not much comfort.

Sukie's breezy confidence was a fraud. It was true that she had performed in front of audiences, in workshops and student productions; but she had been given lines to say and told how to say them; or if she was improvising, everybody else was too, and if nobody understood what you were doing, it made more to talk about afterwards.

76

She said to the others that she was still searching for a sense of artistic direction. But she was not going to be let off.

All that Saturday, all over Medwell Priory and its grounds, there was a brooding air of preoccupation. Solitary rehearsals occupied dormitories and classrooms. The Imaginary Circus bumped and boomed on a tennis court; Sukie's Aunt Helen strutted, puppet-like, beside a playing field; Robin Callender-Smith's life-size puppets conducted a courtship to the accompaniment of a recording of Bolivian music.

Dan strung together a collection of the best of his home-made homespun proverbs—those that had most delighted Lady Simpson and Mrs Calloway and their like—with a linking narrative about working in people's gardens. He also devised and rehearsed a short introduction, to be delivered in the person of Justin Squires, claiming for the proverbs undoubted and well-researched authenticity. It was thin stuff, but he thought it might just about get by. He still felt a little sick at the thought of spouting it in front of them all.

In Sukie's delightful face, towards teatime, he saw an expression of bewilderment which was a very far cry from her usual confident certainty. Nervously he asked her what was wrong.

"I can't decide what to give them," she said.

"But you're a pro. Trained to the minute. Give them a bit of that book you were reading."

"*The Wind in the Willows?* That would be ridiculous."

"Oh," said Dan humbly. "Then mime something."

"There's already three mimes, and that's not counting the circus."

"Four is a nice round number."

"Mime what?"

"The seven ages of man," said Dan wildly, dredging a snippet of culture from his days at grammar school, from his study of the texts set for examinations.

77

"You'd need too many props. Too many changes. It wouldn't work without costume."

"*The Seven Pillars of Wisdom,* the seven sisters of thingummy," said Dan, more and more wildly, "*Seven Brides for Seven Brothers,* the seven deadly sins . . . "

Sukie stared at him blankly. Then her face cleared, and she smiled at him with more than her usual warmth.

"Sloth," she said. "Lechery. Envy. Greed . . ."

Dan was pleased she was pleased; he had not had the sense of pleasing her much in any of their other dealings. His suggestion had not, in fact, been serious. He wondered how she would mime lechery.

He wondered what would happen to him after the following Saturday's performance, when the Symposium would disperse and he would be robbed of its enveloping security. He was no nearer any faintest idea of what to do about Mr Harold Dartie.

They drew lots at teatime, to establish the order of performance. Dan was aghast to find that he was to go on first. Then he was to join the audience so that, on Sunday, he could contribute his helpful criticisms. He did not think anybody would bother to give him any helpful criticisms; all the same, there were going to be some moments when even he could not possibly be inconspicuous.

He went home, fed mother, dogs and birds, and equipped himself to dress up as a rural clown. This was not difficult; they were his normal working clothes, chosen to match the personality he adopted in people's gardens.

He was due on stage at eight, immediately after an early supper.

Marcus Bird, in the early evening, went unusually to the Chestnut Horse. Deac and Chuck, unusually, did not go. They were quite serious about their Imaginary Circus; they would not perform it full of beer.

78

The atmosphere at supper, generally so convivial, was strained; appetites were small, except for Dan's, which was never small, even in the face of what he faced. Only the directing staff were perfectly relaxed; well they might be; they only had to sit and watch, and they didn't really have to do even that. Marcus Bird had some kind of surprise for them all; but the members of the Symposium, excited and inward-looking, were not much interested.

The main hall of Medwell Priory, stone-flagged in imitation of something medieval, narrowed at one end; there were two steps, and a kind of broad landing from which doors opened into classrooms. This landing was used for music recitals, Nativity plays, and the like by the little girls of the Priory school; it was to be the stage for the members of the Symposium. Margot Dean—she of the cropped grey hair and the red trousers—had with the grumbling assistance of George Plummer, the caretaker, rigged up lights on the arch which spanned the two steps. (It was evident to all that, alone of the directing staff, Margot was competent to do this kind of thing.) No attempt at a curtain had been thought necessary. Entrances and exits, if required by the performers, could conveniently be made by the classroom doors. The stacked chairs used by the school for its assemblies were unstacked and disposed in a semicircle. An upright piano was wheeled out of a music room and put by the arch. That was it; it was perfectly adequate. Each performer could go from a seat in the audience onto the "stage" in a few seconds, and return as quickly. Thus there would be fluidity, a nonstop treat of performing art.

This meant that all the members of the Symposium were costumed—those that favoured costumes—when they took their places to appreciate their fellow performers. For manipulating his puppets, Robin Callender-Smith wore black trousers, sweater and gloves. For his modern folk songs, Jeremy Chalice wore his usual prison uniform of blue

79

denim. For their circus, Deac wore a ringmaster's top hat, and Chuck the bulbous nose of a clown. For her dance, Sukie's Aunt Helen wore an immense bow tie, and bright red discs of paint, doll-like, on her cheeks. Sukie herself wore a black leotard which showed off her figure better than anything Dan had seen her wear; it was, indeed, the first thing he had seen her wear which really revealed her figure, a circumstance which made him regret more than ever the peculiar ambiguity of their relationship.

The directing staff were in their normal clothes, though these were not, except in a context like this, so very normal.

Because he was coming on first, Dan did not join the others in the semicircle of folding chairs. He waited, suffering, in one of the classrooms, until Marcus Bird's hand bell (used by the school for fire drill) told him that he was on. He wanted to jump out of the classroom window, and run very fast and very far in any direction. He was dressed in heavy leather boots, corduroy trousers tied below the knee with binder twine, a bright blue flannel shirt without a collar, a leather waistcoat unbuttoned and meant for a bigger man, and his very oldest tweed cap, his grandfather's, the size of a soup plate. There were straws in his hair. He carried a pitchfork. He found it odd to be Dan Mallett dressed up as Justin Squires dressed up as Dan Mallett.

Though what he was about to be subjected to was dreadful beyond imagining, he thanked God that he was there. Stuck tight in the cobweb he might be, but he was safe, for the moment, from the spider.

From his asylum in the classroom, he heard the babble of voices and scraping of chairs which said that the audience was settling.

He said to himself: "I like the people out there. I didn't expect to but I do. If they think about me at all, they wish me well. It doesn't matter how much of a fool I make of myself, because none of them even know who I am, except Sukie, and she only knows where I live." This self-lecture ought to have brought more comfort than it did.

The bell rang.

Dan gulped. To stop his hands from trembling he put them in the pockets of his corduroys; then he had to take them out again, to open the classroom door. When he picked up his pitchfork, it waved like a flag in the wind.

He shuffled out onto the landing, and into the glare of the lights which Margot Dean had hung there. There was a polite sprinkling of applause. Dan found he was not dazzled by the lights; he could perfectly well see all the faces in the semicircle round him. He saw Sukie, looking a little solemn, looking lovely. Deac and Chuck, hairy, sober, prepared to be amused. Robin and Jeremy and the rest, kindly, friendly, expectant, hoping for the best for Dan as much as for themselves.

There was complete quiet. Hands were in laps. It was all up to Dan now. He was on his own. His eye travelled along the semicircle, as though for reassurance, as though for inspiration.

Near the end of the semicircle sat Marcus Bird. On one side of him was Sukie's Aunt Helen, with bow tie and vermilion cheeks. On the other side was Marcus's surprise. It was Mr Harold Dartie, come to see the show.

6

THOUGHTS SWARMED INTO Dan's head like the wild bees that had built a nest in the eaves of his cottage.

Marcus Bird had been that evening to the Chestnut Horse. He had there met and made friends with Harold Dartie, or had seemed to himself to have done so. He saw in Harold Dartie an important ally for the future of the Symposium. He sucked up to him and brought him along, thinking to flatter him by taking him, as it were, behind the scenes of the Symposium, to this halfway event, this working rehearsal.

Why had Harold Dartie come? Simple curiosity? Intellectual interest? In a spirit of mocking? Had he glimpsed Sukie Bush? Or did he know something Dan didn't like the idea of him knowing?

Anyway he knew now. Dan had a momentary hope that Harold Dartie would not recognise him in his stylised, antique rural garments. The hope died as it was born. There was a blink of recognition in Harold Dartie's white-pine face which could be mistaken for nothing else.

Now what? Harold Dartie knew that the witness of the murder of Derek Davis was a member of the Medwell Priory Symposium, temporarily resident at the Priory but presumably leaving in a week. He knew by now, or would speedily know, that the witness was called Justin Squires. He might doubt the authenticity of the name, and of the address Justin Squires had given himself. Harold Dartie would ask himself: What was Justin Squires doing in Medwell even before the Symposium started? What was he doing in Medwell Court in the middle of the night? If he was after the silver, how did he know about the silver? Why hadn't he gone to the police about the murder? That one was easily answered—because he'd pinched four of the five bags of silver.

Dan was still safe from Harold Dartie as long as he was surrounded by the Symposium. Even Dartie would jib at murders by the half dozen. Dan must therefore spend the next week continually in a crowd. How then did he feed his mother, dogs, bantams, pigeons? Take a crowd of the Symposium with him? How else? Blow his own cover with these people? Cause himself to be expelled as an impostor? Lose the protection of their numbers? And what happened at the end of the week, when they all went away? Dan would still be the fly in the cobweb, and the spider would have a clear run.

Wild as a swarm of bees prodded by a broomstick, these and less rational thoughts zoomed round inside Dan's skull, excluding all other thoughts, obliterating all memory of the introductory remarks he was going to have made, all memory of his home-made proverbs, drying him up completely, causing him to stand stock-still with his mouth open, with no idea of where he was or what he was supposed to be doing or why he was carrying a pitchfork.

A cough woke him up. He blinked, and refocussed. He saw that the faces in the semicircle were looking at him oddly, puzzled, worried. He wondered how long he had been standing like a lemon in the glare of the lights. Too long.

He made a gigantic effort to pull himself together.

"Move it, Justin," said a voice. It was Sukie's voice. Dan glanced in her direction, blinking. She smiled encouragingly. She thought he was suffering from stage fright, no more. She thought she was responsible for his being there. Alone of all these people, she knew that he was not Justin Squires, that he had not enrolled as a member of the Symposium, that he was no kind of performing artist and had never intended to become one.

Harold Dartie might already be guessing along these lines—might be guessing that Dan was simply camouflaged as a member of this earnest and high-minded group. His guesses might already have hardened into certainty. He was staring fixedly at Dan. Everybody else was too, but Harold Dartie's stare had a quality which made it quite different from the stares of any of the others.

"Ladies and gentlemen," said Dan, in a tiny high voice which was unlike any of his voices. He realised that this was a totally inappropriate beginning; but this scarcely mattered, since nobody heard it.

"Fur what w'ben about t'receive," said Dan in a better voice, a much better and louder voice, the voice that matched the string round his corduroys and the straws in his hair, "may th'Lard mak' us truly grateful."

One or two faces looked a little shocked. Dan felt a little shocked himself. The words, almost impious, had come out unbidden.

" 'At ben b'way o' interdaction," said Dan, trying to repair his gaffe, "t'whole evenen, nat jus t'liddle ramblens from ol' Zekiel."

The shocked faces did not altogether relax. Dan did not relax. Sukie did not look as though she were relaxing, nor Harold Dartie.

Silence once again enshrouded Dan; he felt as though his head was in a plastic pillowcase. Mentally he tore his way out of it. He was not in one preposterous, unheard-of, intolerable situation, but two. He had to get out of both.

85

He began talking. He had no clear idea of what he was saying, but at least it was coming out in the right accent. He found, to his astonishment, that he was reciting a poem by Robert Louis Stevenson, learned twenty years before as a punishment at school, which he had forgotten he had not forgotten. It was all wrong. He stopped, and sought for something better. There was at least a chance that few of the audience had understood a word.

A proverb. A pithy, pawky bit of country wisdom. He searched his mind. He could not remember a single one.

He stared at his pitchfork for inspiration.

He said, " 'Ere ben thray sarts o' pitchen-fark. Ben a sart wi' tu prangs, ben a sart wi' three prangs, ben a sart wi' fower prangies."

So what? Where was this leading? Nowhere.

"Ben same like folks," he went on hopefully.

But they weren't. No trace of sense could be made of this ridiculous proposition.

"A-ben usen thicky pitchen-fark fur t'kill spiders," he said.

What they called a Freudian slip.

The audience was silent, attentive, thoroughly puzzled.

Dan was beaten. Under the grim glare of Mr Harold Dartie, under the kindly, uncomprehending eyes of the Symposium, homespun philosophy fled away and stayed away.

"Hark!" cried Dan, and fled into one of the classrooms behind.

It was inglorious, pathetic, contemptible. Dan Mallett the mocker of authority, the scourge of gamekeepers, the wild fox of the woods, was incapable of doing what eight-year-old children did all the time. He had not thought of himself as an abject coward, but now he had to. The bright classroom smelled of chalk dust, floor polish and fear. It was not the fear of the generations of little girls who had sat at the rows of desks. It was Dan's fear, entirely new to him, of making a fool of himself in public.

86

The window stood wide onto the golden evening. Dan went through it, dropping into a flowerbed full of ground elder. He thought that he could, perhaps, face the Symposium the next day; he could not do it that day. Facing Mr Harold Dartie was another problem.

He went softly round the side of the big ugly house, keeping out of sight of the windows of the hall. They would be waiting for him to start again; or perhaps to admit that he couldn't start again. Harold Dartie would be waiting for him. No, probably not. Harold Dartie knew Dan had recognised him, as well as Dan knew he'd been recognised. After Dan's humiliation, Harold Dartie would ask questions about him, which he could hardly have done before without sounding strange. He could show interest in a non-performing artist; he could be frankly and openly curious. Where does the fellow come from? What does he do for a living? What sort of bloke is he? Does anybody here know him well? Everybody looks at Sukie. She knows him better than anybody else. Well, Miss Bush, tell us all you know. What would Sukie tell? Maybe nothing; maybe just enough to put Dan's mother and dogs and birds and Dan himself in the most frightful danger. He had no idea what to do; but he must make a very good plan immediately. He sat down, out of sight, to ponder. There was a time for action and a time for thought; this was a time for both, but the thought must precede the action.

Sukie imagined that Justin Squires was looking at his script, or taking a shot from his flask. There was a murmur of conversation round her, a mixture of tolerance, pity and contempt. She herself felt a mixture of all three. She wondered for the hundredth time what the funny little man was doing in the set-up, dropping his whole usual life for two whole weeks just because she smiled at him, if that was why he had done it. Obviously performing was agony to him. Sukie had never much suffered from stage fright herself, but she knew people who actually vomited almost every time they had to go on stage. Some of the best actors were like that. Some of the worst, too. Nobody had ever been worse than Justin Squires. It was a shame, because that hayseed act had the potential to be pretty good, kind of a British Will Rogers, if it only had a script and somebody who could get up and deliver it.

The minutes dragged by. Sukie began to wonder if her odd new property was coming back. Maybe he was cowering in a corner. Maybe crying. Maybe huddled in the fetal position. Maybe blacked out.

"Marcus," she said, "maybe I better go see if he's okay."

"Good idea, sweetie. Tell him not to worry about anything. He needn't go back on if he feels he can't, but he must rejoin us."

Sukie nodded and stood up. The stranger, the new squire of Medwell, half rose as though he intended to follow her. But he sat down again.

Sukie went to the classroom. She went in and shut the door behind her, in case any scene that was going to be played was something that ought to be in private. She saw the open window, and realised that Dan had gone out of it. She ran across and leaned out. There was no sign of him. She scrambled through and dropped to the ground, landing among a lot of plants she hoped were weeds.

She straightened and looked round. The evening was washed with gold. With her back to the house, she could see only grass and woods. The ancient tangles of the woods were touched with points of gilt; everything had a luminous quality; everything looked half asleep. The softness of the light blurred the edges of things. It was completely unlike the relentless clarity of Florida light, or that which she had been seeing in Southern Europe. There was something to be said for the place; Sukie could see how people got to like it.

There was no sign of Justin Squires or anybody else. She

had the lovely evening to herself. Presumably he was okay, if he jumped out of windows and went across lawns. She ought to get back to the Symposium. She felt a sudden and extreme disinclination to go indoors, to sit in artificial light with a crowd of people, to breathe their breath and be nudged by their shoulders. She was still a little worried about Justin Squires, especially as she had got him into this. She didn't know what she could do about him, when she didn't know where he was.

Dan sat, fairly comfortably, in the middle of a clump of shrubs. He pictured his expulsion from the Symposium—some kind of ritual, with a hollow square of performing artists. No. They would let him stay, sure enough, however much they despised him, because they wanted the rest of his money. So, for another week, he was still safe in the bosom of the Symposium. He would just have to be very, very careful when he went to feed his household.

Mr Harold Dartie was sitting in the Priory, certainly trying to find out about Dan; since he was there he was not somewhere else. He was not in his room at the Chestnut Horse, and he was not at Medwell Court. Those therefore became places it was possible to visit, to search. To search for what? For anything that revealed something about Harold Dartie; for anything that could be used against him; for anything that helped in any way at all. Dan felt that, for once, he wanted any help at all, from any source. He wanted it within the next seven days.

The front bedroom at the Chestnut Horse was not a serious possibility. Harold Dartie was not a man to leave his room unlocked, and Ted Goldingham was not about to give Dan the keys of his customers' rooms. Dan knew where Ted hung the keys, on a board behind the bar. An earwig could not get to that board without being seen, not now with the pub full of people. If Dan started a fire, emptied the pub . . . No. If it was a little fire the pub wouldn't empty, and if it was a big fire he wouldn't be able to get upstairs to the bed-room. To be burnt to death solved his problems, but he hoped there was a better way.

More and more stuff had been going into the Court, as reported by gossip in the Chestnut Horse, itself reported at the Priory by Deac and Chuck and the others. It was being spread around the house under Mr Dartie's direction. The stuff might include filing cabinets, or desks with drawers that could be opened. The security guard was still there, but still it was all a lot more possible than the Chestnut Horse project.

There might not be another chance like this. Probably Harold Dartie was on the verge of moving into his fine new house, and once he had done so it was not a place Dan cared to burgle.

He would stay to the end of the performance there in the Priory hall. At least, it would look very odd if he suddenly got up and went out, and odd would be the last thing he would want to look. When he did leave, he would obviously go to the pub where he was staying, not the house he hadn't yet moved into. That was a fairly safe assumption, and one that had to be made.

Dan decided to go home, change back into the clothes he wore for expeditions of this kind, and get the key of the flower-room door that he had long ago been given by Peggy Bowman. He would walk to the Court, not being seen by anybody; there was no way to be invisible on a bicycle. As soon as it was full dark, he would go in and peep round. It was odds against him finding anything useful; but there might be something, and it would be crazy to pass up this one chance of finding it.

The whole prospect was odious, exhausting and alarming.

Obviously, Sukie thought, he would go home to that crazy Hansel-and-Gretel cottage on the other edge of these woods. Home to be comforted by his mother, and maybe by

90

all those dogs and hens and pigeons. Feeling a little responsible, even a little motherly herself, Sukie decided to make sure he was all right, which she could do by seeing him—no need to talk to him, no need to reveal herself as a snooper—which she could do by going to the cottage.

A black leotard was a funny thing to wear for prowling through the woods, but nobody was going to see her.

With relief Dan changed out of his clownish clothes, into the ones which chose themselves for burgling houses. His equipment was a pencil flash and the flower-room key; after a moment's thought he pocketed also his home-made cosh, which he had often carried but never used. He reminded himself to make another blackthorn stick with lead in the handle. He drank some whisky, pacified his dogs, and tried to pacify his mother.

A sudden illness was the best story he could think of, to explain his abrupt disappearance from the Symposium. Not the galloping gargles; some other. It was very lame; nobody would really believe it, but he thought he would have to say something.

Sukie sat watching the cottage without knowing quite why she was there. It was a lot pleasanter in the woods than it was in the hall of the Priory. It was prettier. The atmosphere was sweeter. The birds made a better noise than the Symposium did. The cottage did have a kind of crazy charm; it was not like any dwelling in Florida, or any that she had seen on her travels all over Europe. Probably it could not exist anywhere else. Probably "Justin Squires" could not exist anywhere else. Sukie guessed he was an unusual specimen even here—a man who seemed like a normal yapping middle-aged middle-income Brit, but who lived in something made out of gingerbread. Perhaps middle-aged was a little hard; but he was certainly nearer to middle age than to her own age.

Where did middle age begin? Her own seemed a very great distance off.

She felt pleasantly guilty, playing hookey from the Symposium. She was relieved about Justin; he was not sobbing, or fainting, or in a catatonic trance. She glimpsed him once or twice, going in and out of the cottage; she heard voices, though not what was said. She wondered again what he did for a living, and how he could stop doing it, suddenly, for two whole weeks without telling anybody or asking anybody.

He came out of the cottage, wearing dark pants and a dark turtleneck. Sukie saw him lock the door and hide the key behind something. She imagined he'd head back for the Priory, but to her surprise he went off in the opposite direction.

Idly—not deeply interested but mildly curious—she wondered where he was going. She wanted to stay out of doors, on this perfect evening. She wanted something to do, to occupy her mind.

She followed him.

Dan was in no hurry. It was obvious that the Symposium's proceedings were going to last a long, long time, and that Harold Dartie would stay with them, and that when he did emerge it would be to go to the pub. The sky was darkening. There was nobody about. If there were courting couples, they were preoccupied; and they were as little anxious to be seen as Dan was.

Often Dan was obliged to lope across the countryside at exhausting speed. Now he could allow himself the luxury of strolling. At that moment it was the one luxury his circumstances offered; he made the most of it. Uncut corn gleamed white in the gathering darkness; a few birds rustled among the dead leaves under the hedgerows; a white owl wavered out of a wood to hunt in the stubble.

Dan crossed into the Medwell Court estate by a ha-ha at the bottom of a pasture. He strolled between sleepy bullocks. He could just see the dark bulk of the house and its outbuildings, a quarter of a mile ahead. No light was showing in any window. All that could be heard was the placid breathing of the bullocks, and the weird shriek of the hunting owl. Dan's footsteps made no sound on the cropped grass of the pasture. There was a slight clink as, in his pocket, the flower-room key nudged against the metal of the cosh. He moved the cosh to a different pocket. He went slower and slower as he neared the house, looking and listening. He climbed out of the field into the paddock below the house where Major March had sometimes grazed his horses. The bullocks, which had followed him as bullocks do, shifted and breathed heavily and rubbed against the fence.

Dan began to prowl along the paddock fence towards the side of the house where the flower room was.

Sukie had no idea where Justin was leading her, or what he could possibly be doing. All sorts of ideas crossed her mind. He was meeting a girl? Somebody's wife? He was committing a crime? Burglary? Surely not. He didn't have the guts for anything like that. Nobody who went to pieces as completely as he had, there in front of the Symposium, was liable to do anything as risky as breaking and entering.

She felt a much keener curiosity about her funny little friend than she had ever admitted to herself. What *was* he up to?

He went slow, so it was easy to follow him. Her black leotard was the best possible camouflage. Her sneakers made no sound on tarmac or grass. She kept only near enough to him not to lose him. Even if he turned round and faced in her direction, she would be invisible. Meanwhile it was still a whole lot pleasanter to be out in the open, under the warm sky, being breathed at by the incredibly lush countryside.

It was a funny route Justin picked, but he seemed to know where he was going. It was lucky he was going so slow. Was

93

that because he couldn't go any faster? Because he liked smelling the flowers in the hedges? Because he needed it to be properly dark before he did whatever he was planning to do?

He led her up hill and down dale, along the edges of fields, over fences and through hedges. They never once went along a road, although they crossed a road or two. Sukie became completely disoriented; she had no idea in which direction the village lay, or the Priory, or the gingerbread cottage. Suppose Justin was not going back? Suppose he was going to hole up in some other gingerbread cottage, or meet someone in a car who'd whisk him away over the hill, or catch a bus? She supposed she could face a night in the open, but she didn't relish the prospect. It was borne in on her that boredom, curiosity and a liking for the fresh air had maybe landed her in a horrible predicament. Her only guide was that funny little man strolling along in front of her. What he was her guide to, God alone knew.

He climbed a fence, and started across a big grass field. In the incomplete darkness, Sukie saw that the field was dotted with cattle. She had very little experience of cattle. She was inclined to be wary of anything big, with horns. She trotted up to the fence, keeping behind some bushes growing close to the field. She saw him; she saw the cattle. They were showing signs of following him. He was obviously unconcerned about them. They were some kind of cattle that didn't charge you and gore you and trample you. British cattle, as harmless as Justin himself. She climbed the fence. Using a couple of the cows as cover, she crossed the big field after him. Still, as far as she knew, he never looked back the way he had come.

She never looked back, either. She was concentrating on keeping Justin in her sights. Her eyes were by now thoroughly accustomed to the darkness. In it, black against not-quite-black, she saw a big house a long way ahead. His objective, obviously. What house? Whose house? What did he want there? If he went in and got swallowed up, what about her?

He climbed out of the field, leaving a crowd of cows. Under cover of the cows, she followed him to the fence. He was standing absolutely still; she thought he was looking towards the house; she thought he was looking and listening. He might be a lover or a burglar or an arsonist or a vandal or a Peeping Tom, or a guy who was going for a stroll in the dark, and happened to come to this place.

He moved on, very slowly now, towards the black bulk of the buildings. She crawled through the fence, and waited until he was well on across the smaller field they were now in.

He was up to no good. What sort of no good was he up to? What was a soft, nervous little creep like him doing prowling up to a dark building on a dark night?

The buildings were all dark. There might be people sleeping inside, or people inside who were not sleeping, but Sukie had the strong feeling the place was empty.

Justin seemed to think so too, because he went right up to the side of the house, moving very slowly. Sukie lost him against the blackness of the building, but she knew more or less where he was. The night was now absolutely still. The cows were quiet, and the bird that had been screaming was quiet. Moving as slowly and silently as Justin had, Sukie got nearer to the house. She crouched behind a big stone urn, on the edge of a paved terrace.

She wondered what the hell she thought she was doing, creeping about in somebody's garden in the dark. She was not really scared. There was nobody around except Justin, and there was no way she was ever going to be scared of him. She was not doing any harm. If she was breaking a law, it was only a little law. She could, if it came to the point, give an exact and truthful account of her reasons for being there—curiosity, suspicion, concern, stuff like that—which would sound creditable rather than the reverse.

Peeping through some plants which were growing in the urn, she picked up Justin against the wall of the house. She thought he was by a door. In the absolute stillness of the night there was a tiny scratching noise, a kind of click. Her eyesight and hearing were very good, or she could neither have seen him nor have heard those small noises. She thought he had opened the door. How could he do that? Was there a girl inside who had left it open for him? She was waiting for him in pitch darkness? Or did the British leave their doors unlocked at night?

She lost sight of him. He had gone in through the door. There was no subsequent click. He had left it ajar behind him.

Now what? Sukie decided to wait and see. It was all she could do, until he came out again and led her back to familiar places. It was all she could do even if he didn't come out again. She decided against following him into the house. She was not that brave, and she didn't want to get into any trouble in a strange country. She waited, not uncomfortable, quiet as a mouse; she began to will Justin to finish his business, and come on out of there, and guide her back to the Priory.

She was grabbed from behind, by hands that felt like steel. Her arms were twisted round her back, awkwardly, painfully. There was a grip on her wrists like a tourniquet. She was hauled to her feet. She began to scream, but even as she began, a hand was clamped over her mouth. She struggled. All that happened was that her arms were more painfully twisted behind her back. She was as helpless as a rag doll in the hands of a giant. She had difficulty breathing with the big hand over her face. Her arms and wrists hurt badly, and the hand on her face hurt her.

She was half pushed, half carried, across the flagstones of the terrace, to the side of the house and the door which Justin had used. The door seemed to be ajar. Her attacker used her as a ram, to push the door open. She was lifted inside, into dense darkness. The door banged shut behind them; her attacker must have kicked it shut. He was not troubling about how much noise he made.

He made more noise. He shouted out, in a strong, deep, harsh voice.

He shouted, "Squires, or whatever your name is. Come here and start talking. Or I'm going to break this girl's fingers one by one."

7

THE HAND WENT AWAY from Sukie's face. She screamed.
Now that they were indoors her attacker made no attempt to
stop her screaming. He wanted her to scream, to bring Justin. She knew she ought to stop screaming, but she could
not.

He was gripping and twisting both her wrists with one
hand. His fingers felt like steel cables on her narrow wrists.
The only effect of struggling was to hurt her wrists.

A light went on, a bright overhead light, revealing white-
painted walls, an uneven stone-flagged floor, a high ceiling,
some doors, an arch. The switch was evidently by the door
they had used. The man was standing a foot or two away
from the door, with his back to it.

Now that he had a hand free he could turn on lights, and
break her fingers, and use a knife or a monkey wrench or
whatever else he had.

The giant behind her shouted again: "Squires! You heard
what I said? This girl has ten fingers. I'll break one every
thirty seconds."

The deep, harsh voice reverberated along the stone pas-
sages. When its echoes died away, the only sounds were
Sukie's own shuddering sobs.

"I'm starting with the little finger of her left hand," shouted the man, his breath blowing through the close-cropped hair on top of her head.

Sukie screamed, in terror of the imminent and excruciating pain.

And the world exploded.

The man, and Sukie with him, was suddenly driven forward as though by a giant hand. The grip on her wrists slackened. She pulled away, but not far enough. The man crumpled, falling against her, bearing her violently to the stone floor. He half fell on top of her. She was winded. Her face and breasts and legs and belly were hurt. She thought she had broken bones in her legs and arms, and broken her ribs and back. She could not move for being winded, and for the weight of the man across her.

She twisted her head painfully, and saw that the door was wide open to the night, and in it stood a small, dark-clad figure tucking something away into the pocket of his pants.

It was Justin.

He pulled the inert body off her, rolling it away. She never saw the face. She saw grey hair, a nondescript tweed jacket. They meant nothing to her. She was too shocked for curiosity. She just wanted to get away.

Justin pulled her to her feet. She struggled to breathe. She thought she had not broken any bones, but her whole body felt like one vast bruise. He pulled her out through the door, turning off the light as he went. He shut and locked the door.

"Can you run?" he said.

"No," gasped Sukie, with the first proper breath she had succeeded in taking.

He supported her with his arm round her waist. His arm felt surprisingly strong. His arm felt reassuring, and with its help she managed to trot beside him. They went not back the way they had come but in a different direction. They were in a yard among outbuildings, then among disciplined little trees. Though it was pitch dark, Justin seemed to see in the dark, or to know his way exactly.

100

"He won't be asleep very long," said Justin, as though apologising for making her hurry.

They trotted on through the dark, on grass and then on a gravel driveway, through lodge gates and onto a road, and through a hedge and into a field of stubble.

"We can slow down," said Justin, "but we'd better keep moving."

He kept his arm round her waist. She no longer needed it physically but she needed it morally.

Sukie stopped dead, struck by a thought which, being so obvious, would have struck her before if she had been less terrified and less amazed and less bruised all over.

"After he'd broken all my fingers he would have killed me," she said.

"Yes. Well, as a witness you wouldn't have done his case much good. And after I'd shown him a rabbit hole he would have killed me."

"A rabbit hole," said Sukie stupidly, making no sense of this at all.

"Why on earth were you there?"

"I don't know. I followed you."

"And he followed you. I can understand why he followed you, if he thought you were following me, but why did you follow me?"

"I don't know. Fresh air. I was tired of being indoors with all those stupid people. I guess I was curious."

"As before. I hope you liked my cottage. My mother doesn't."

"How did you knock out a huge man like that?"

"It's a trick I learned a long time ago. It was lucky he was standing where he was, or I don't quite know what I would have done. As soon as I heard your first yell, I picked up my feet and went through the house and out the other side and back to where I started, to that door. So then I reckoned he must be facing inwards, away from the door. Silly to shout to a closed outside door, when you think the bloke you're shouting to is inside the house. And when you shout, to

101

make yourself heard all through a big house like that, you naturally raise your head. There was a good chance that the back of his head would be the first thing the door hit."

"You hit him with the *door?*"

"As I say, it's an old device. Stood the test of time. Somehow the hinges double your strength. I suppose there's a reason in mechanics for that. I knew more or less where he was, when he shouted out how many fingers you had."

"You opened the door pretty violently."

"Middling hard. It's a good big heavy door. I do like these old houses."

"Oh," said Sukie, "oh."

"He's a sturdy fellow, that. Most men would have gone base over tip. He just lurched a bit. So I smote him with the jawbone of an ass. When a man's off balance you can deal with him easier. Nothing to it, really. He simply wasn't expecting me to be behind him. Of course there was the possibility that he had you between him and the door."

"Oh," said Sukie.

"When he said, 'This girl,' of course I didn't know what girl. I speculated. Very quickly, of course. I guessed it might be you, because as far as I know you're the only girl who's followed me these last few weeks."

"How did you know I followed you? Okay, okay, you heard me. You didn't hear me this evening."

"We didn't go through any woods this evening. No telltale crackle of twigs. You did very well. So did Mr Dartie."

"I'm fed up calling you Justin. What's your name?"

"Dan."

"Dan what?"

"I've probably told you too much already. Why didn't you come in, when you found out where I lived? I could have given you a better drink than that thin stuff Marcus Bird pours out."

"I would have been embarrassed. I was snooping."

"Curiosity went thirsty. You'll know better next time."

"Hey, I haven't thanked you for saving me. I do. I truly do. You were insanely brave."

"Forget it. Or better, remember it. Let it be a warning to you. I'm letting it be a warning to me."

"Against what?"

"Being followed without knowing it."

"Who was that man?"

"Ah," said the small brown man about whom she was so greatly revising her opinion. "You didn't see his face?"

"No. Who is he?"

"If you went to the police, you couldn't give a useful description of him?"

"Big. Grey hair. Tweed jacket."

"That's three million people."

"Powerful. A sadistic bastard."

"That's two million people. You can't identify him. I wonder if that's a good thing or a bad thing?"

"Who is he?"

"I wonder," said the man who now called himself Dan, which might or might not be his real name, "where the security guard was. Not there, obviously. Our friend knew that, obviously."

"Maybe that was the security guard," said Sukie.

"Maybe. Excessive devotion to duty."

"How did he know your name? Your phony name?"

"Gossip in the pub. No secrets in a place like this. They probably all know your name too."

"He said, 'Come here and start talking.' Talking about what?"

"As we cut the conversation short, we may never know."

"Why do you live in that crazy cottage?"

"East, west, home's best."

"But you make like an officer in a bank. Like Robin and Jeremy and those."

"Protective camouflage. Of occasional value. Not the real me."

"What is the real you?"

"Something like a wood louse, really, crawling out of old timber."

"How can you just drop everything for two weeks?"

"Nothing much to drop. No large career. No awesome responsibilities."

"Why did you suddenly join that racket at the Priory?"

"At your suggestion."

"All right. I had a reason. What was your reason?"

"Cultural stimulation. New horizons."

"You're not gonna tell me a goddam thing?"

"The less you know, the better."

"I can walk okay now," she said crossly, and removed his arm from her waist. Then she remembered that he had just saved her from torture and death; she took his hand, and replaced it round her waist. It would not go any further. Whatever he had saved her from, she was quite clear about that.

"I'll go to the police first thing," she said.

"Um," said Dan. "With a full account of tonight's doings? It won't help them catch a man you can't describe."

"I see you don't want me to. Would it get you into trouble?"

"A mite of trouble. I did go into that house."

"Why did you go into the house? What house is it? How do you have a key?"

"Gift. Sort of keepsake. Part of my collection."

"Were you going to rob the place?"

"No. I was hoping to find some evidence."

"Are you a detective?"

"Do I look like a detective? Where's my regulation grey raincoat?"

"I guess you're some kind of crook. After tonight, I don't want to get you in trouble. But a bastard like that can't be allowed to get away with a thing like that. Every one of my fingers!"

104

"I hope he won't get away with it. But there's nothing you can do, at this moment, to stop him doing so. There must be a quarter of a million men in England, at a conservative estimate, who exactly answer the fullest description you could possibly give the police."

"I was raised to have a civic conscience."

"What are we going to tell them all? What am I going to tell them, and what are you going to tell them?"

"Well, what?"

"I was taken ill. You've been looking after me. I ate a toadstool in the wood. You've been holding my head."

"That's a lousy story."

"Yes," admitted Dan. "Your turn, then."

"You ran away, out of embarrassment, and I chased after you to bring you back. Only it took a long time to persuade you."

"Element of truth in that. I wonder if our friend followed you all the way from my cottage?"

"I guess he must have."

"Oh, dear."

"He was going to kill us both, after you showed him a rabbit hole . . ."

"But we thwarted his plans."

"You did. There must be something very special about your rabbit hole."

"Yes, an unusual specimen. Not your ordinary rabbit hole."

"Listen," said Sukie, "I'll keep quiet about your going into that house, but I can't keep quiet about everything. I won't. For one thing, I have to explain the mess I'm in."

"Are you in a mess?"

"Bruised. Scratched. Filthy from that floor. My leotard ripped. I have to explain all that."

"You took a toss over a root in the woods."

"I did not. A guy tried to mug me, and you saved me. Not with a door. I won't tell about the door. You deserve to get

105

credit for what you did. Especially after what happened, the way that made you look. I mean, think what everybody must have thought of you, standing there with your mouth open. They have to be told there's another side. And then if you want help they'll help you. You deserve being helped. I didn't think you did, but now I know you do."

"How could they possibly help me?"

"By being around. You didn't kill that guy. If he's so anxious to see your rabbit hole, he'll try again. Break my fingers, or something different. Break your fingers. Maybe, between all of us, we can do quite a lot more than just be around. Deac and Chuck are pretty tough, and there's some high-grade brains in the group. But of course, if anybody's going to help you, they have to know what it is they're helping."

"Snag there," said Dan.

"Do you have something hidden in that rabbit hole? Drugs?"

"Good gracious, no. I wouldn't even know what a drug looked like."

"Jewellery?"

"No such luck."

"Or maybe pictures? Are you blackmailing him?"

"I wouldn't dare."

"I just understood something. God, how slow I've been. You joined the group to be protected against that guy. To kind of hide in the crowd, to be surrounded by people. That's why you came along the moment I asked you. I thought . . ."

Even in the dark she looked embarrassed.

"I think I know what you thought," said Dan. "You were right. You were the other reason."

"Oh . . . As long as you stay in the middle of the group, you're safe. But the group breaks up at the end of next week. Then what?"

"That thought has been bothering me. Occasioned a qualm."

106

"We have a week to solve this. You do need help. You have friends, you know."

"I don't want anybody taking risks," said Dan. "I don't want anything like tonight, not ever again."

"I didn't know what I was getting into. Now we're warned. Are we nearly home? I need a bath with a lot of disinfectant. I hope the water's still hot."

They rehearsed their story for the members of the Symposium. Sukie was entirely determined that Dan should get public credit for rescuing her. He had to give way on this. In return, she promised to keep quiet about his having unlocked and entered the house, and about the secret which her attacker had so very much wanted to share. She would say nothing about the rabbit hole. Thus the length of their absence would be explained, and the condition of her leotard. And, she said, Dan would be forgiven for flunking out on his performance.

They agreed that her attacker was a would-be rapist, since she was clearly not carrying anything worth robbing. As to where the attack had taken place, they agreed to be vague. It was dark; they were both strangers. Sukie would go on calling Dan "Justin," and she would keep quiet about his cottage.

She continued to urge on him the merit of coming clean about the whole thing, to her anyway, and maybe to the whole group. He continued to demur. There was something terribly law-abiding about almost every member of the Symposium, for all they were performing artists; one or another was practically bound to feel obliged to go to the police. Jim Gundry would like that, but Dan's mother wouldn't.

Sukie said there was nothing wrong with her except bruises. She would be stiff in the morning. She yearned for that hot tub.

They got back to dither and consternation. Marcus Bird had been on the point of calling the police. Their joint story, now well rehearsed, elicited cries of horror, sympathy, admiration. As Sukie predicted, Dan's abject failure to perform was forgotten in the heroic aura with which she now surrounded him.

Sukie went off to have her bath, unnecessarily supported by her Aunt Helen. As soon as she was out of the way, Dan asked Marcus Bird about Mr Harold Dartie. Yes, he had been curious about Justin Squires; he had wanted to know where Justin came from and what he did. And shortly after Sukie had followed Justin into the classroom, he had mumbled some excuse and left.

"Effect of me," said Dan.

Marcus Bird visibly agreed. Sponsorship of the Symposium, in future years, by the local magnate had seemed, there in the Chestnut Horse, so very probable. Now it was grossly improbable. A lesson had been learned. On any such future occasion, a proved and seasoned performer must go on first. If that meant cheating on the lottery, cheat on the lottery.

Deac and Chuck wished they had been there, to deal with the mugger-rapist. Sukie's gratitude would have taken a practical form. Obviously it wouldn't with Justin. He wasn't that kind of guy.

Some of the ladies of the Symposium looked as though a rapist on a warm summer night would have been far from odious to them.

Dan was aware, more strongly even than before, of general goodwill from this strange group. Sukie was right—he did have friends. At least, Justin Squires the assistant bank manager did. Dan, as Dan, was enjoying friendship under false pretences. He had enjoyed a good many other things under false pretences, but this time his conscience was a little bothered.

He knew no more about Harold Dartie, but Harold Dartie knew a lot more about him.

Although Dan was tired, he lay awake for a long time in the little bed in the little upstairs dormitory.

108

His thoughts swung between Sukie and Harold Dartie.

It had been nice having his arm round Sukie's waist, even though he was sorry for the reason. It was the nearest they had come to any physical contact. At first it was necessary—she needed his help to get along at the speed they had to get along. When she no longer needed it, she took it away. And then she put it back. That might have been construed as an invitation, but Dan was quite sure it was no such thing. It was a way of saying thank you, an appreciation of the way he had got her out of a very nasty spot. She somehow made that as clear as though she had said it out loud. He was never going to get anywhere with her—and especially now that she had seen him illegally entering somebody else's house. It was a very, very great pity. Though he was still far from understanding her, he liked her more and more.

She would not say the things she had promised not to say. He knew that much about her. It was one of the things he liked.

The only thing he liked about Harold Dartie was that he seemed to do his own dirty work. He had done his own murder, and stolen his own silver, and done his own strong-arm stuff. He didn't employ a gang; anyway not for those sorts of things; anyway not here. If there was a threat to Dan's mother, of the kind that Sukie suffered or any other kind, or to Dan's cottage or his dogs or birds, precedent indicated that Harold Dartie would do the threatening. That was bad enough. But it was better than half a dozen heavies from the back streets of Portsmouth. It became advisable to put a kind of guard on the cottage, in the sense of having somebody there who'd see and report any atrocities. Dan himself couldn't hang around there on his own. But with enough friends he could. He had the friends. He wasn't sure how much he could ask of them—they were here to do a particular interesting thing, and they wouldn't be overjoyed at the prospect of doing a quite different and very boring thing. Keeping watch on the cottage would be very boring indeed, unless it became unpleasantly exciting. It would mean they all knew about his cottage. It would mean they all knew he was a phony, a crook. They'd have to know a bit more about that. His thoughts came back to an earlier point: they were just too law-abiding to give him the help he needed, if they knew enough about him to see how much help he needed.

Putting it baldly, if they didn't know enough to help they wouldn't help; and if they did know enough to help they wouldn't help.

He went to sleep with no answers to any of the questions he was asking himself.

One floor up, Sukie too was wakeful. Several parts of her were pretty sore. But what really kept her from sleep was the realisation of the terrible thing she had unwittingly done to Dan, if that was his name, and Sukie thought it probably was.

That horrible powerful man, who had been quite ready to torture her, wanted very badly to get hold of Dan, to force something out of him, to kill him. He had not known where Dan lived. Now he did. He knew because Sukie had led him there. Presumably he had been waiting and watching somewhere near the Priory. He had seen Dan disappear, but maybe lost him. Then he had seen Sukie going into the wood, looking as though she knew where she was going, going after Dan. So Sukie had led him to the cottage, and now it would be that old woman's fingers which would be broken.

Sukie choked at the thought of something so obscene. But it was realistic. The fingers that had held her wrists had a totally merciless quality.

It was Sukie's responsibility to save that old woman from the consequences of Sukie's own meddling, her curiosity, her impertinent snooping.

Sukie went to sleep with her decision made, and a clear idea of the method.

8

DAN CAME DOWN TO BREAKFAST at eight-thirty. It was not the sort of breakfast that he liked or usually had, his taste and his requirements tending to piles of bacon and eggs and fried bread, sausages, mushrooms, potatoes, sometimes a chop. The Symposium's diet was far different. What there was, Dan ate; his appetite had been sharpened by the events of the previous night.

He thought there were empty places at the breakfast table. Some of the performing artists, perhaps, were exhausted—lying in late after the emotional drain of performing.

He helped to clear up breakfast. Then, inconspicuous as always, he slipped into the edge of the woods. He was no nearer working out how to guard all that was his from Harold Dartie; in the meantime he thought he had better make sure his mother was all right.

He went through the wood very quietly and cautiously. It was an obvious possibility that Harold Dartie would visit the cottage, with equal stealth. It was what Dan would have done, in Harold Dartie's place—spied out the place, seeing if there was a lever there he could use. If he came, he would

111

sure enough see the lever, which he might well not have done the previous evening. His plan would probably then be to get Dan's mother out of the cottage and into a car. He would have to use force to do that. He had plenty of available force for manhandling a shrunken and severely arthritic old lady. When he had got her safely away and hidden somewhere, he would get a message to Dan at the Priory. The telephone would do. And then Dan would have to tell him where the silver was, which would be annoying; and then he would kill Dan, as the witness of his murder of Derek Davis, which would be still more annoying.

As Dan approached his cottage, moving like the shadow of a mouse, he was astonished to hear the music of a guitar; and with it, after a few bars, a reedy voice upraised in a song Dan did not know.

Whatever was going on, it had nothing to do with Harold Dartie, unless he had enlisted some very rum recruits.

Still moving with infinite caution, Dan moved nearer. Probably there was no need for caution; no hoodlum bent on abduction and torture would serenade his intended victim. But nothing was lost by caution, and Dan was completely puzzled.

He saw Jeremy Chalice, North London librarian, composer and performer of modern folk songs; Jeremy was sitting with his back to a tree, five yards from the cottage, his guitar in his lap. From where he was sitting he could see two sides of the cottage, and fifty yards of the rutted lane which led from the cottage to the road. He was working. In his lap also he had a pad. After trying a chord or two to a phrase of the song he was writing, he made a note on his pad. He could do that as well here as anywhere, but why here? Dan was completely astonished.

There were further surprises for Dan as he slowly emerged from the bushes. Leaning against another tree, with another sort of pad, sat Isabel Robey, the middle-aged widow from Littlehampton who, like Sukie's Aunt Helen,

112

performed interpretive dances, but without such impressive force of character. She was not at the moment being a performing artist, but the other sort of artist: she was doing a drawing of Dan's cottage. And a little way away, by the fence behind which Dan's dogs were kennelled, Maxwell Piper, the Reading dentist, was reading a book.

Dan advanced, wondering if they were mad or he was. Jeremy Chalice looked up from his notebook and gestured a greeting.

"Hullo, Justin," said Jeremy. "Been sent to join the sentries?"

"Sentries?" said Dan. "*Sentries?*"

"Good Lord, you of all people must know about it."

"Sentries?" repeated Dan stupidly.

"Your girl friend has pressed the panic button."

"Girl friend?"

"Sukie. I would have thought she would have told *you.*"

"I haven't seen her today."

"Well, we blooming well have. That's why we're here. Not a bad idea, actually, to get away from the mob for a couple of hours. Sukie swears that the old gargoyle who lives in this hovel is in some kind of danger. It's the lad you tackled last night. What she realised, thinking about it later, was that the bloke you tackled wasn't after her at all. I mean, she wasn't his primary target, she was just getting in the way. The primary target was the old girl. Sukie says she must have something valuable in there, though judging by the exterior it hardly seems likely. My own suggestion is that the owner wants to evict her, clean the place up, and sell it as a second home to somebody from London. We all said, go to the police. Sukie already had."

"*What?*"

"Rang them up first thing this morning. The police said they'd already been in touch with the old girl. They said, if she thought she was in danger, the thing to do was move out, at least until the danger went away. She's got a family. She

113

doesn't need to be here all alone, she just insists on it. My mother's exactly the same, actually. It makes problems, but one does understand. Independence is precious. But the police don't see it that way. They can't mount a twenty-four-hour guard on this place. So Sukie said we must. It's no hardship, in this weather, and we can get on with our thing as well here as anywhere. Of course what we're losing is the post-mortem on last night's frolic, but between you and me, I don't seem to mind about that as much as I should."

"Good gracious," said Dan.

He glimpsed his mother for a moment, staring malevolently out of the window of her bedroom. Then her lined, white, unforgiving face disappeared. Dan assumed she would pretend not to notice the incongruous strangers who were surrounding her cottage. If any of them tried to talk to her, she would pretend to be deaf-mute, as when the police asked her questions about Dan's movements.

Sukie had made herself responsible for putting a guard round his mother. It was her fault that Harold Dartie (only she didn't know it was Harold Dartie) knew where Dan lived; so, she reasoned, it was up to her to do something about it. She had recruited these decent people, who were there partly because of the undoubted strength of Sukie's character, and partly because they didn't want an old lady robbed or mugged or evicted. The story she had told them was a bit thin, a bit ridiculous, but as a matter of fact it wasn't far from the truth. She had just left bits out, such as Dan himself, the bits she'd promised she'd leave out.

Dan thought: That is a marvellous girl. He was consumed with admiration and gratitude: and, concomitantly, with regret.

"We had a most unexpected visitor a few minutes ago," Jeremy Chalice went on. "Our guest of last evening. The new owner of the big house. I forget his name. The big bloke Marcus Bird brought along, hoping he'd turn into a kind of local patron for the future. I don't know what he was doing, visiting a place like this. Being the benevolent squire, I suppose. But he didn't go into the cottage. Just had a look round and went away again, as though he'd forgotten why he came. Affable fellow. If I were a sculptor I'd want to do his head. Great strength in repose. Might have been a model for Donatello."

"Oh, easily," said Dan politely.

He wondered about his evening routine. He wondered about the nights. He wondered about the following week. He wondered if Sukie had any more plans.

"We're being relieved in time to get back for lunch," said Jeremy. "Or so Sukie faithfully promised. Changing of the guard. The next detail will bring a picnic. I simply can't understand why Sukie didn't tell you about any of this."

Dan understood. Sukie had decided that her plan was the right plan, but she thought Dan might not think so. She must have gone round to all the dormitories early in the morning, briefing all the members of the Symposium. Breakfast time would be too late, because Dan would be there vetoing the scheme. And that after the bashing she had taken! Everything he found out about her increased his admiration, and his regret.

Harold Dartie had not wasted any time, either. He must have recovered pretty well from being bashed in the back with that huge oak door, and then knocked out with a cosh. He was durable. He could take it as well as dish it out. It was extremely lucky that Sukie's sentries were already in position when he arrived. Would he have realised they were sentries? Presumably, since they were there the morning after the evening's frolic. Unless he thought some of the members of the Symposium did their homework here as a regular thing.

Knowing where Dan lived, he would know by now who Dan was. He would know all about him. He would know from Jim Gundry, the village bluebottle, that Dan Mallett was the biggest villain unhung—notorious poacher, suspected thief—who ought to have been behind bars years ago. It didn't seem to Dan that it terribly mattered, Harold Dartie hearing this account of him. It didn't matter that Harold Dartie could expose "Justin Squires" as an impostor. What he couldn't expose him as was an intruder in Medwell Court on the night of the murder of Derek Davis. That knowledge was Harold Dartie's personal property.

He had come to the cottage, found it surrounded by witnesses, and gone away again. Had he really gone away? How far had he gone? Was he even now watching them from the middle of a clump of hazel? He was a big man to be hiding in bushes; well, he could hide in a big bush. He was good at shooting security guards, and following people across country in the dark, and grabbing and threatening girls; he was a hard, violent, effective operator; it was to be assumed that his brain worked and that he knew how to hide in a bush.

Dan had taken an absurd risk, coming alone to the cottage from the Priory. He would not take the risk of going back again alone. He would go escorted by Jeremy Chalice, Isabel Robey and Maxwell Piper; he would go after the changing of the guard. He sat down near Jeremy, and watched him writing and composing a modern folk song.

> The girl was young and light and slim,
> These things they didn't bother him.
> He set on her, and hurt her sore,
> To rob or rape or something more . . .

Jeremy's new song was about the attack on Sukie, and Dan's intervention.

> But there came by a valiant guy—
> Thanks be to God the guy was by . . .

Jeremy didn't have his facts quite right, but it was a most touching tribute. Dan had never, as far as he knew, had a

116

song composed about him before. Though touched, he was embarrassed. He got up and strolled away, to look at Isabel Robey's drawing of his cottage, which had also never before been artistically celebrated. But the drawing was not as good as the song.

The morning dragged. His mother's face did not again appear at the window. He was not sure if she had seen him. It was better not to go in. That would probably have enraged his mother, as upsetting her morning routine, and would certainly have declared to the others his special relationship with the cottage.

Dan stretched himself in the sun, and dozed until the relief came. He was safe from a sniper in the woods, if Harold Dartie wanted his silver back, and it seemed he did. Dan was alert, although he was almost asleep. He was like a dog dozing in front of a fire, which is on its feet and barking in a second if there is a small noise which it thinks might be threatening. He could hear nothing beyond the rustling and peeping of birds in the trees, the twanging of Jeremy Chalice's guitar and his pleasant, reedy tenor, the scratch of Isabel Robey's pencil on her sketch pad, and the turning of Maxwell Piper's pages. But he reminded himself that the sentries thought they were guarding only his mother; they did not know she was his mother, and they did not know they were guarding him too.

At twelve-thirty the relieving sentries arrived. They were led by the formidable figure of Sukie's Aunt Helen, in midcalf pink pants and a big hat. Dan wondered how much dancing she would do, and what his mother would make of that. Following her came Robin Callender-Smith, the puppeteer; he carried his sewing box, a roll of pieces of fabric, and the papier-mâché head of a new puppet. It was to be an afternoon of dressmaking. Third was Geoffrey Farland, an estate agent from Exeter and a player of antique wind instruments. There was something in the breast pocket of his prison uniform that looked like a piccolo; he was carrying a big plastic cold box. Cheerful greetings were exchanged. There was some discussion about the nature of the threat to the old lady in the cottage, and the reason for it. Jeremy Chalice's theory of an eviction, stated before breakfast, was finding general acceptance, on the grounds that there could not possibly be anything of value in the cottage.

Dan thought of the rabbit holes in the woods behind him.

"I still want to know what happens when we go away next Sunday," said Sukie's Aunt Helen.

"Me too," said Dan.

"My guess is young Sukie will have organised somebody to take our place," said Robin Callender-Smith. "Don't you think so, Justin?"

"Indeed," said Dan. He did not think he had ever before used "Indeed" as an answer to a question. It came of being addressed as "Justin."

Still no reference was made, by way of the six, to the fiasco of his performance the previous evening. None had been made at breakfast. Probably it had been discussed at the post-mortem, which he had missed. He was glad not to have heard that.

Escorted by Jeremy, Isabel and Maxwell, no less effective for not knowing they were escorting him, Dan went back to the Priory for lunch.

He saw Sukie for the first time that day. She smiled; then she looked defiant.

"Thank you very much indeed for your arrangements," said Dan.

"You're not mad?"

"Of course not. It's a huge load off my mind. But what about tonight?"

"Is there some place in the house three people could sleep? I don't think it should be less than three."

"No," Dan agreed. At night, knowing Harold Dartie, he would have preferred eight or ten. "I've often slept on the floor in front of the kitchen range."

"That's it, then."

118

"Um. There might be a problem."

"It should be three guys, I guess."

"That solves one problem, but not the problem I meant."

"Your mother."

"Set in her ways. Bundle of prejudice. Distrust of strangers."

"You'll have to talk to her. Explain."

"She doesn't like explanations from me. She hasn't believed a word I've said since I was about four."

"If you talk to her like you talk to me, you don't actually ever say anything."

"Best not. Open old sores."

"Look, either she's got to agree to have three guys sleep in her kitchen, or they'll have to creep in after she's asleep."

"Impossible. I can't do it, on my own."

"I'm doing my best."

"I know you are. It's a very good best."

"Let's eat."

"Yes," said Dan, who after a morning of almost total inactivity was ravenously hungry.

After lunch, out of earshot of the others, Sukie said, "You have chores at home in the evening, right?"

"There is rather a zoo. They demand their rations."

"You can't be all on your own there then, any more than at any other time."

"The prospect is less than delightful."

"So we stand in a ring around you. So everybody knows where you live."

"It's been bothering me, that."

"Why? Nobody cares where you live. These people are not snobs. A lot of them might envy you, living in a quaint place like that. Isabel Robey thinks it's darling."

"I signed a false name. I said I came from . . . I can't remember where I said I came from."

"Seems to me a lot of these names are false. Can you believe 'Jeremy Chalice'?"

Dan laughed. He faced the inevitable. He saw that Sukie

was right, but he was not happy about it. She was right that only by declaring himself to the rest of the symposium could he safely feed his mother, dogs and birds, bring in firewood from the range, and fill the water butt from the well. She was right also that these people were not snobs; they would not expel him from the Symposium because he lived in a small and ancient cottage under the trees at the edge of the wood; some of them might, as she said, even envy him his cottage, and the life that went with the cottage. The fact remained that he would be unmasked as a fraud, a phony who had lied his way into the Symposium for some reason unexplained, unexplainable, and presumably discreditable. He had taken advantage of the good nature of them all; he had abused their trust.

He had not been quite right, brooding in the middle of the night: they were helping him without knowing that he needed help or why he needed it. But that was because Sukie had been so ingenious and so persuasive.

However much they despised him as a performer—as a non-performer—he had a feeling of being liked in the Symposium. They liked Justin Squires as Justin Squires; it was not the same as Lady Simpson condescendingly liking Dan Mallett as Dan Mallett. It was altogether better. It was something he would be sorry to lose. It was, no doubt, better than losing his fingers and ears and nose, which seemed the inevitable alternative.

"All right," he said.

"Good boy."

Four of them went to the cottage with Dan in the early evening: Deac and Chuck, as inseparable in sentry duty as in imaginary circuses; Francis Mordaunt, the Guildford teacher and Symposium illusionist (his was another name in which Sukie said she disbelieved); and Sukie herself. They would relieve the three who had been on duty since tea time; they would themselves be relieved in time to get to the pub before it shut.

120

"I have, hum, a kind of statement to make," said Dan bashfully, as they crossed the grass towards the edge of the wood.

They looked at him with interest but without surprise. Sukie had warned them that they were in for a revelation.

Dan said that he was not Justin Squires, that he was not an assistant bank manager, that he did not come from wherever it was he had said he came from. He told them what he was called and where he lived.

They all stopped, as though astonished, as though this amazing and shocking news could only be absorbed by people standing still.

The three men began to laugh. Glancing at them nervously, Dan saw nothing obviously derisive or hostile in their laughter.

"To tell you the truth," said Francis Mordaunt, "I much prefer the name Dan Mallett to the name Justin Squires."

"Dan Mallett," said Chuck. "I believe we heard people talking about you in the pub."

"All too likely," said Dan.

"Ted, the guy who runs it. He said the local cops had been trying to get you for years."

"Oh," said Sukie.

"Ted Goldingham exaggerates terribly," said Dan. "Jim Gundry and I are old friends, in a manner of speaking."

"But why?" said Chuck. "Why not say, 'My name is Dan, I live in this village, here's my dough.' Marcus Bird wouldn't have worried, as long as the dough was for real."

"Yes, why?" said Francis Mordaunt.

"Yes, why?" said Dan to Sukie.

"Well," said Sukie, "it just happened that other way. Justin Squires had a ticket to the thing. Dan didn't. Justin paid his deposit."

"That is a point," said Francis Mordaunt, laughing again.

It seemed they admired his gall. They were not shocked at his deception, even the Guildford schoolmaster. They understood his wanting to attend the Symposium, since they

121

themselves had wanted to attend it. It was not, to them, and never had been, the strange caprice, the perverse extravagance, which it had at first seemed to Dan. They did not forget that Dan had saved Sukie. They now fully understood and forgave his dismal showing the previous evening.

Dan found to his astonishment that he was better liked and more admired than before.

The threat to himself, his mother, his cottage? Dan found that he thoroughly disliked deceiving, in a new way, these people who had become his good friends. But it would not do to tell them the whole truth. The removal of four carpetbags of Harold Dartie's silver had seemed to Dan, and still seemed to him, less morally odious than almost anything he had done in all his life. But it would not do to make these people accessories after what was, strictly speaking, a crime. Accessories also after his failure to report a murder and describe the murderer.

"Jeremy Chalice was about right," he said. "Somebody wants my cottage so badly he's prepared to do anything to get it. It's as though he knows there's a gold mine under it."

This was ironic, he thought. There was a silver mine almost under the cottage.

"Violence and intimidation to secure possession," he explained, "same like slum landlords in inner cities."

"For God's sake, get the cops," said Deac.

"They wouldn't believe a word of it. Not till my mother had her arm broken or I had my head bashed in."

"Wasn't Sukie's experience last night enough to convince them?" said Francis.

"They wouldn't believe there was any connection," said Dan. "A beautiful girl gets scragged. Attempted mugging or rape. How can you turn that into somebody trying to get possession of a house?"

"Who wants the house?" asked Chuck.

"We don't know. Approaches from lawyers, principal not named. We refuse all offers. It gets through to them our refusal is final. That triggered last night. We were safe until then."

This story seemed to Dan so good that he almost believed it. It did hold together. If there were loose ends, inconsistencies, incredible bits, they did not immediately strike his listeners. They swallowed it completely, and they were very indignant.

Dan felt doubly guilty.

With the somewhat confusing assistance of the four in the know, Dan told the three sentries then on duty at the cottage who he was and what they were guarding against. Their reaction seemed to him the same. There was no moral disapproval of his having cashed in on someone else's deposit, and none of his having used an assumed name.

Many hands made light work of drawing water and stacking firewood, of giving the dogs their run, and feeding the bantams and pigeons. There threatened to be too many cooks spoiling the broth of Dan's mother's dinner.

The argument about whether three strange men should sleep on the floor in the cottage kitchen was resolved by sheer weight of numbers. Old Mrs. Mallett was simply shouted down. Dan had never seen such a thing before. The police had never achieved it, although there had sometimes been as many policemen in the cottage as there were performing artists. Dan's mother went to bed in a rage.

Deac and Chuck made it to the Chestnut Horse before closing time. They came back pretty sober and pretty pleased with themselves. They said they'd solved the problem of protecting Dan (they still, absent-mindedly, mostly called him "Justin") and his mother and his home.

"We met that guy Dartie," they said, "the new lord of the manor. We told him about this eviction caper. He was pretty mad. He said he had a big staff, gardeners and gamekeepers and fellows who dig ditches and stuff. He said they'll take over guarding the place. He said any hood who tries to come

123

busting in, any hour of the day or night, will wish he'd stayed home and taken up embroidery. He said they'll start tomorrow."

"That's wonderful," said Sukie. "That solves everything."

9

OH, IT WAS SO LOGICAL, so obvious. Oh, how sensible, how wise, how practical, how far-seeing, how caring the two young Americans had been. Mr Harold Dartie, squire of Medwell, had said and shown how concerned he was for the people of the village and the surrounding countryside. In the bar of the Chestnut Horse and in the post office, in bus queues, the waiting room of the doctor's surgery, the garage, in all the places where the village met to talk, it was agreed that Mr Harold Dartie was to be liked, respected and trusted. This message had come loud and clear to the members of the Symposium. And it was obviously true that he had fine, strapping country fellows working on his estate.

The solution was so inescapably right that it was amazing none of them had thought of it before.

Mr Dartie's sturdy labourers would collar the heavies if they tried anything; get from them the identity of their employer; go to the police with proof of harassment and intimidation; and secure the permanent safety of the Mallett household.

The members of the Symposium had not really wanted to prolong their sentry duty until the end of the week. They

125

had not really wanted to sleep on the kitchen floor of the Malletts' cottage. Sedentary and middle-aged, they had not wanted to tangle with the man described by Sukie. It was the sort of thing Mr Harold Dartie's estate workers would be much better at. All parties, in fact, benefitted from the new arrangement, not least Dan and his mother.

Oh, how relieved he must be! Oh, how easy he could now sleep!

"I don't think," said Dan, "you're going to believe this."

"Try me," said Sukie.

His previous revelations, which he had been so deeply reluctant to make, had not been received as he had expected. But it was not a crime not to be an assistant bank manager. It was not a crime to assume somebody else's identity, if you made no money by doing so—if, as in this case, you actually spent money by doing so. In spite of what his mother said, it was not a crime to live in that cottage. But he now had to tell Sukie a bit more of the truth. He thought that, as he said, he would have a job making her believe it. In order to make her believe that the new situation was truly frightful, he was going to have to tell her far more than he had ever told anybody.

It came of being in a team. Dan had never been in a team before. Much as he was coming to like the members of this peculiar team, he hoped he was never in such a large alliance again.

"Well, now," he said, "it's about that man who grabbed you last night. No. Wait. I'll start in a different place. As you probably saw, my mother has pretty bad arthritis. That's really the key to the whole thing."

Sukie looked at him blankly. Dan saw that the connection was, indeed, far from obvious.

"Bear with me," he said. It was a phrase he was certain he had never used before. It pleased him. "Bear with me," he repeated, since if there was any pleasure to be got out of the

126

situation he might as well get it. He explained about his mother's arthritis, about the recommendation of Dr Smith in regard to a hip operation, and about his mother's adamant refusal to go into a public hospital.

"You'd think she was too small to be so stubborn," said Dan. "You'd think she was too frail."

"I understand so far," said Sukie. "But I don't understand why you're telling me."

"Central to the whole situation," said Dan. "Key to the whole affair."

He spelled it out so as to invest his position with unassailable morality. He invoked filial devotion and the relief of suffering. He laid it on a bit thick, partly to overcome Sukie's scruples, partly because he was embarrassed about coming to the point.

He mentioned the cost, when last quoted to him, of the hip operation done privately, of a private room in a hospital, of X-rays and the anaesthetist's fee and the aftercare.

"Don't you have health insurance?" said Sukie.

"I did when I worked in the bank. It's one of the things that went out with the bathwater. So financing my mother's operation is a problem that has to be approached in, hum, an unconventional way."

"I knew you were a crook, but I didn't know why. I don't think I'm going to accept any of this."

"What would you do, placed as I am?"

"I would have kept up the health insurance."

"Yes."

Laboriously, Dan explained the rules he had made for himself, his self-denial in the matter of the choice of victims, his refusal to take anything from anybody who needed it, from anybody who was not already self-branded as some kind of cheat or bully.

Sukie looked a little wooden. She was not impressed.

Ploughing on, Dan gave her a heavily edited account of the night of the murder.

"Wait," said Sukie, frowning. "Wait. You say the guard was a friend of yours?"

"Acquaintance," said Dan. "Congenial bloke. Widely popular. Lonely job, sitting in an empty house."

"You went there that night to keep him company? Or to burgle the place?"

"Betwixt and between," said Dan. "Voyage of exploration."

"You could have saved yourself a lot of hassle by going straight to the police."

"There were objections to that. Course wasn't open to me. Matter of my mother's hip. Of course, at the time, I didn't know who the murderer was."

"I get it now about the rabbit hole."

"Local version of health insurance."

"Who was the murderer?"

"I nearly walked into his arms, in the Chestnut Horse. I don't know when I've had such a nasty turn."

He knew she was not ready to believe him. The softening-up process had not worked.

He told her. She did not believe him.

"I can easily prove it," said Dan mildly, "by having us both murdered. I don't quite see how else I can prove it. Unless—I wonder if you'd recognise the back of his head?"

"No. I was in shock. How can you expect me to believe that a guy who can afford a place like that would do a thing like that? Why would he take the chance, when he already has so much dough?"

"I'd say he can afford a place like that because he's made a career of doing things like that. None of the people in his address book had ever heard of him. He's somebody else, like me. I was trying to find out who he was, the night before last. Look, if it wasn't the owner who grabbed you, how did he know the guard wasn't there?"

"There's a thousand ways he could have known."

"Hum," said Dan, realising that this was true.

128

"People *like* the guy. Seems the whole village likes him."

"He's bought them."

"Marcus Bird likes him."

"Marcus Bird was hoping he'd buy him too."

So they wrought, over cups of instant coffee, after all the others had gone to bed. Sukie was convinced that Dan was lying to her—he had, after all, been less than frank with her from the moment of their meeting—or that he was simply wrong, confused, misled by a similarity. To her his proposition was so grossly improbable that it was impossible. He realised with a shock that this was because they were in England. In America it was possible that an oil magnate or a beef baron or a railroad mogul could also be a ruthless bandit. It was even probable. Folklore said so, and it was what a lot of films were about. But an English squire, owner of a gracious Georgian mansion and a fine estate, benevolent neighbour of a village with a name like Medwell Fratrorum—such a man had rosy cheeks and a heart of gold.

Without Sukie's leadership, there would be no Symposium presence at Dan's cottage. (Even with it, there was a doubt.) And without that presence . . .

The battle was resolved by a totally unexpected intervention. Sukie's Aunt Helen came into the common room. She was dressed in a flowing, floor-length cotton robe; her entry had an air of interpretive dance, but actually she was just coming into the room.

She said, "I have a confession to make. Sukie Mae, I accepted from your mother the charge of supervising your moral welfare while you were in my care. That was, of course, a condition of your coming with me. That gives me not just the right but the duty of supervising your behaviour. It has been evident to me, as to all of us, that a relationship developed between yourself and the gentleman we thought of as Justin Squires. As to the precise nature of that relationship, my friends here and I agreed that nothing was liable to occur of which I could not in conscience give a

129

reassuring account to your mother. The discovery that Justin Squires concealed the identity of this gentleman did not, of itself, give rise to any disquiet in this regard. However, my friends here have, as you know, been in the habit of dropping in at the tavern. It was there this evening, as you also know, that they discussed with those present the uncomfortable and even dangerous predicament in which this gentleman finds himself. General discussion of Dan Mallett, there in the bar, elicited a consensus, among those who knew him, that Dan Mallett was a dangerously immoral man with an undoubted, if incomprehensible, attraction for persons of the opposite sex. Among inhabitants of the village present there was unanimity on this point. As you know, my friends reported publicly one part of the conversation they had. They reported privately to me this other part. They felt it their duty to do so. It was not so much that they felt obliged to give me a specific warning, as that they believed they were obligated to put me in possession of facts relevant to my stewardship, if I may so express myself."

Sukie's Aunt Helen did not always express herself at such length, or in such measured periods; but she quite often did. It depended on the seriousness of the subject; this subject was very serious.

"It was further borne in upon me," she went on, "that the two of you had been alone together in this room for an hour and a half. You would be reasonably confident that all the rest of the party was asleep. I lay in my bed pondering where duty lay. Eavesdropping is distasteful to the discriminating spirit. But was I not in danger of hiding behind this instinct, as an excuse for shirking my duty of surveillance? So I reasoned, and so found myself outside that door. That is all my confession. I wronged you both. You, Dan Mallett, may be all that your neighbours say, but you have treated this little girl in my charge with honour, and I shall not demur henceforward to trust you as I have trusted you in the past. You, young lady, have acted with a discretion and a purity about which it will be my pleasure to report to your

130

mother. But you have shown yourself obdurate, prejudiced and closed-minded on the topic of your debate here tonight. Why should Dan Mallett have told you what he did, confessed to you as he did, put himself in your power as he did, if not motivated by what he perceived as imminent peril? Why should he invent incriminating revelations about himself?"

"He might have been just wrong, Aunt Helen," said Sukie rebelliously. "Just confused."

"He has given us, over the last week, no reason to suppose that he is either myopic or muddle-headed. If he confidently identifies Mr Dartie as the murderer of that unfortunate man, then we can proceed on the hypothesis that he is right. If he is, in the event, proved wrong, no harm is done; if we have not shared our suspicions, no reputation is smirched. As a precaution, we will send a team in the morning to relieve those presently on duty. Mr Dartie will not therefore be permitted to abduct Dan Mallett's mother, thus compelling him to reveal the whereabouts of whatever it was he stole. Incidentally, I am a little disturbed, Dan, that you were not more frank with us, that you allowed us to believe in the fiction of a threatened eviction."

"Hum," said Dan, almost too surprised to speak. "Yes, sorry about that. I expect you can understand, though."

"You had only to explain about your poor mother's hip. And as to her reluctance to commit herself to the public ward of a general hospital, I so well understand. It is a feeling I wholeheartedly share. Well, I will overlook the degree of deviousness of which you have been guilty, and I am confident that I shall persuade my colleagues to be equally lenient. We will discuss the whole matter in open session in the morning. We have until noon next Sunday to unmask Mr Dartie as the murderer, provided, of course, that we are correct in our assumption that he is. Our endeavour will be to achieve that end without compromising your own status, Dan."

"Thank you," said Dan. "Thank you very much."

131

"We have assembled here a variety of skills which we may contrive to make relevant. Those of a musical or terpsichorean character may prove of doubtful utility, but you will find we shall pull our weight in other ways. Now it is time we were all in our beds. We shall need healthy minds in healthy bodies for the challenge of the days to come."

That amazing woman gestured imperiously for Sukie to rise and leave. Sukie obeyed with a meekness Dan had never before seen her show. In the door she paused, turned, and looked at him. He could not read her expression, but he thought he could guess what was on her mind. Not so much that Harold Dartie had now been officially adopted as the Symposium candidate for the Medwell Court murder; more that reported talk in the pub about himself and all those girls. He knew Sukie had not seen him in that light. He was not sure, even now, what light she did see him in; indeed, the more he saw of her the less he knew what she thought of him. Now, perhaps, she didn't know what to think.

Dan said good night to her aunt, who knew exactly what to think about everything. He went to bed himself, almost immediately, still groggy with astonishment. He did not at once see how the talents of puppeteers, modern folk singers or players of medieval flutes were going to unmask a murderer. But perhaps the "open session" promised by Sukie's aunt (at the thought of which Dan cringed) would produce a plan.

They had six and a half days.

Another team of three was sent to the cottage early in the morning. They were to relieve the sentries of the night, who might be expected to be stiff after sleeping on the kitchen floor. They were to make their own breakfast, and that of Dan's mother, when they got there. It was evident to Dan that none of the three wanted to go, but they could not stand up against Sukie's Aunt Helen. Nobody could. Dan continued to be amazed by American females.

Dan's mother would, presumably, consent to having her breakfast made for her. His dogs would consent to being let out, and his bantams and pigeons to being fed.

The three night guardians came back to the Priory in time for a late breakfast. There had been no invasion of the cottage in the hours of darkness. Old Mrs Mallett, they reported, was angry at having three strangers sleeping in her kitchen, but she accepted that they were friends of her son's and that they meant no harm. It was as clear to them as it was to Dan that their relief would be set to work. But the new three would have to chop firewood with their chins on their shoulders. Harold Dartie was certain to arrive sometime during the morning.

The open session commenced just before ten o'clock, as soon as breakfast had been cleared away and washed up by those whose turn it was, and who were paying such a lot of money for the privilege of performing these tasks. All the members of the Symposium attended, except the three on guard at the cottage, and all the directing staff. Sukie's Aunt Helen took the chair, without being nominated, seconded or voted for. She explained the situation, accurately if incompletely. There was at first general incredulity, like Sukie's; Deac, Chuck and Marcus Bird were particularly unwilling to believe that their new friend was a cheat and a murderer. Sukie's Aunt Helen appealed to Dan. Bashfully, he corroborated her account of the murder. He explained that this was what had actually induced him to join the Symposium; he was already more or less forgiven for that.

"Why didn't you go straight to the police?" asked Margot Dean, her trousers seeming redder and her grey hair closer-cropped than ever.

"Hum," said Dan. "It comes down to my mother's arthritis."

They all looked at him as though he was mad. Dan began to relive his argument with Sukie; the difference was that he now had a powerful ally.

133

"I am satisfied that it was impossible for Dan to go to the police," said Sukie's Aunt Helen. "I ask you all to accept my assurance in that regard. I may add that I am known by those close to me as a staunch upholder of the processes of law."

The point was not accepted without a struggle. Dan was amazed that these deeply respectable people even considered accepting it; he realised, with a renewed shock, that it was not so much Sukie's Aunt Helen's eloquent earnestness that convinced them, as the fact that these people liked him. It took a bit of getting used to, and he had not yet succeeded in getting fully used to it. All this togetherness was still too new to him. He saw merits in it. He did not see how they could help, but he saw that they wanted to try. He found himself moved. He heard himself saying "thank you" several dozen times.

It was not clear where Sukie stood. Her face, usually expressive, gave nothing away, and she said nothing. Dan had not spoken to her since her aunt had swept her off to bed the previous night.

After an hour it appeared that, under the leadership of their dynamic chairperson, the Symposium had undertaken to mount a team effort to unmask the Medwell Court murderer. The meeting therefore moved to a consideration of ways and means. Sukie's Aunt Helen found it a good deal more difficult to impose procedural control. Debates became altercations. Some of the suggestions were frankly ludicrous.

"It seems to me mandatory," said Robin Callender-Smith in a rare moment of general silence, "that we do not publicly declare ourselves convinced of the guilt of the man Dartie until all trace of doubt has been expunged. We must be more than morally certain. We must have proof. That must be our objective. The point I make is that until we have achieved it we must be circumspect in the last degree. Because if we come out and say he did it, and he can convince other people that he didn't, he can throw the book at us."

"Sue the pants off us all," said Deac.

This contribution had the effect of complicating the debate about methods, to a point at which no proposal received the support of more than two or three voices, or, as in many cases, the single voice of its proposer. Dan, a convert to the idea of teams, found his new faith wobbling. It seemed that thirty people were as incapable of having a good idea as one was. The morning wore on, performing arts forgotten.

At twelve-thirty another team of three was despatched to the cottage, with a picnic and a bottle of Soave. The returning team reported the arrival, at ten, of Harold Dartie in a car. He had come alone. He had not brought the posse of strapping labourers of which he had talked in the pub. This lent some colour to the theory—by no means yet unconditionally accepted—of his villainy. He must have been surprised to find Symposium members still on guard and intending to remain; he hid his surprise. He may have been chagrined; he hid his chagrin.

"He only has to wait until noon Sunday," said Sukie's Aunt Helen.

It was not afterwards clear by whom the name *Hamlet* was first uttered. By some it was ascribed to Isabel Robey, by some to Maxwell Piper. The effect was electric. These clever and literate people all, immediately, grasped the essence of the plan expressed by that one word. Dan did himself, having been dragged through the play at grammar school.

Enthusiasm was tremendous. The idea was near genius. From a meeting which had become almost Arabian in its fragmentation of policies there emerged a sudden and almost total unanimity. It was highly gratifying to Sukie's Aunt Helen.

The whole crime would be re-enacted, by the combined efforts of the Symposium: the insuring of the silver; its delivery to the Court; the installation of Derek Davis; the mid-

135

night arrival, by ladder, of Harold Dartie; the arrival soon afterwards of Dan; one murder and one attempted murder; the hijacking of the silver. Harold Dartie, assuming himself an honoured guest, would be narrowly watched. It couldn't fail. The king in *Hamlet*, now that everybody came to think of it, was rather like Harold Dartie, though it was true that Dan was a good deal unlike the prince.

There were obvious roles for puppeteer, folk singer, interpretive dancers, mimes: less obvious ones for medieval woodwind instruments or an imaginary circus. But nobody was going to be left out. A lot of hard work was faced with enthusiasm.

Dan tried to raise a lone voice of dissent. He tried to point out that it worked in the play because Claudius already felt guilty. Harold Dartie would not look guilty because he did not feel it. Dan's objection was ignored. It was almost said out loud that he was unqualified to contribute to the discussion. Everybody was in love with the idea. Everybody was convinced it was the inescapably right solution to their problem. Everybody saw also that it was the optimum way for this particular group to use its talents to save Dan and his mother, and to bring to book a particularly brutal murderer.

Dan realised, with a feeling of despair, that after all he was going to have to do the whole thing himself.

10

As he pondered unhappily on his probable and imminent violent death, it occurred to Dan that, of all those present at the great debate, Sukie alone had contributed nothing. It could be argued, to be sure, that her Aunt Helen had sufficiently represented the family; but it was Sukie who had been attacked by Harold Dartie, Sukie who had initiated the Symposium surveillance of Dan's household, Sukie who had received the various stages of Dan's confession. She was in the middle of the whole thing. One would have expected her to hold, and express, strong views. Her silence was unusual and surprising.

It had been surprising that, all the first week of the Symposium, she had sought him out and stayed close to him. It was now surprising that she did not. She was at the other end of the room, and she stayed there. He caught her staring at him. He could not read her expression. She might be staring because of what Dan had told her, or because of what her aunt had told her, or for some other reason.

Dan found that he missed very much having her beside him.

Perhaps she would mime Greed in the Symposium's concerted effort to unmask Harold Dartie. Dan wondered if she had a spare leotard; her other one had suffered considerably from the events of Saturday night.

In the early evening, the sentries were relieved by other sentries, who would themselves be relieved by the night watch. The dogs and birds were fed. Dan cooked his mother's supper, while she watched in resentful silence. Dan had hoped Sukie would come to the cottage with him, but when he looked for her she was not to be seen.

Harold Dartie was not to be seen, either, all that long hot day. He had accepted the impossibility of violence—until after lunch on Sunday.

The villain-exposing drama to be presented on the Symposium's final night should have had, perhaps, a single directing intelligence. This was generally recognized; but there was disagreement about who the writer-director should be. What emerged during Tuesday was that half a dozen people thought they not only should be, but were, in charge of it all. A number of different programs were thus being simultaneously prepared. As far as he knew, Dan figured in none of them. This was the only blink of light in a situation otherwise entirely murky. Sukie's company would have been another blink of light but she was still keeping clear of him.

The ceremony of the Nightcap took place as usual, as though nobody was about to be unmasked, nobody about to be murdered. As usual, Jeremy Chalice with his guitar led the singing of what had become the Symposium song.

"Montparnasse of the West Countree . . ."

At that time of day, even more than any other, Sukie had been close to Dan. Close, though never touching. Now she was, as during the debate, at the other end of the room. And, as during the debate, she was staring at him. Dan joined in the singing, bashfully, which he had not previously done. Sukie stared at him as he sang; she did not sing herself.

Deac and Chuck came back from the Chestnut Horse.

They had not seen Harold Dartie. Nobody had; he had gone away for a day or two. Ted Goldingham said it was business.

The Symposium speculated about Harold Dartie's business. Enlisting heavies? Planning a bank robbery? Something on those lines. It was evident to Dan that he was now entirely believed by them all; they were sure he had seen what he said he had seen, at Medwell Court at two in the morning; they were sure it was Harold Dartie and not some other who had grabbed Sukie. It was a new experience for Dan to be believed by so many people all at the same time.

Sukie might be the exception. There was no way of knowing what she thought.

Wednesday morning. Dan woke early, to a perfect dawn. He went downstairs quietly, and out onto the stretch of grass beside the Priory drive. The grass was laced with millions of cobwebs, dew-wet, lit by the first pale rays of the sun. Dan did not go far from the house. Harold Dartie had left the Chestnut Horse for a day or two; he might have come no farther than this.

On the grass, a little way off, he saw something he had heard about but never seen. A small flock of pied wagtails, like perky, strutting waiters in their smart black and white plumage, were extraordinarily busy about something. They *were* being waiters. They were all feeding one young cuckoo, who sat fatly in the grass going *chizz-chizz-chizz*, giving orders to them all, demanding more food more quickly. The young cuckoo did not look like any other bird, or behave like any other bird. He was a Harold Dartie among birds, greedy and ruthless.

Dan knew that there were more male cuckoos than female, which he did not think was the case with any other bird. Either there were a lot of bachelors, or the hen birds consorted with several cocks. Dan's father always said it was the latter; he said the hens were tarts, which was why they never bothered to bring up their own chicks. She'd lay an egg on the ground, pick it up in her beak, and pop it into a hedge sparrow's nest, or a pipit's, or a wagtail's. In colour her egg would imitate the eggs of one of these birds, but very often she got it wrong, and put an imitation hedge sparrow's egg into a meadow pipit's nest. Still the unfortunate foster parents seemed not to notice the difference. If there were already other eggs in the nest—the proper eggs, which belonged there—the mother cuckoo got rid of them. Sometimes she ate them, sometimes she simply threw them out onto the ground. It made no difference to the chicks inside the eggs. If there were more eggs when the cuckoo chick hatched, he got rid of them. If there were nestlings, he got rid of them. He went *chizz-chizz-chizz*, and seemed to hypnotise his hosts with this wheezing, unmusical command. Anyway they all always dropped everything to look after him; they fed him and fed him while their own chicks were dying within sight and earshot. And when he was fledged and active and out of the nest, he still ordered his non-stop day-long meal, and they still obeyed. And sometimes, as now, other birds were pulled into his retinue, and the cuckoo had not two devoted slaves but five or six.

This might make the cuckoo seem helpless. Really it showed just the reverse. He took it easy because he was boss. He was actually very self-reliant. When other birds flew off south for the winter, the children went with their parents, to be looked after, to be shown the way. But this chap's parents had likely already set off, while he would hang around here for another month, and then set off for Africa all alone.

The cuckoo starting south had more sense of direction than Dan had. It had more time too.

When he went in for breakfast, Dan thought that the extraordinary sight of all those wagtails feeding the young cuckoo should have made him forget his troubles for a minute. But it had had the opposite effect. It had reminded him of them. Derek Davis was a wagtail chick sacrificed to the greed of the intruder. He himself had very nearly been an-

140

other, and so had Sukie. Harold Dartie's insurance company was a wagtail ministering to his greed; probably all those people in his address book were doing it too, although it seemed they knew the cuckoo by another name.

Sometimes something in the natural world about him had given Dan useful ideas; he had taken hints from dragonflies, rooks and honeysuckle. All the wagtails and cuckoo did was depress him.

He ate his healthy breakfast bran in a despondent mood.

Thinking of the breakfast he really wanted made him think of all the south coast eateries in Harold Dartie's address book. Out of eighty or a hundred, eleven had no telephones. They had had; they no longer did. All disconnected for failure to pay the bill? That was an impossible coincidence.

Dan had abandoned his attempt to find something out about Harold Dartie from all those names and addresses, from all those Tandooris and Takeaways. Why had he? It had been folly to give that search up just because the people he tried to talk to spoke inadequate English, just because Harold Dartie, in dealing with them, used a different name. It was odder and odder, the more Dan thought of it, that the owner of Medwell Court should carry about a sort of registry of the cheapest kind of eating place; that the murderer of Derek Davis should do so. The search must be resumed. There was only one way to resume it.

The events of the previous few days had demoted Dan from his status of the previous week to his real status; but in an opposite and more important sense they had promoted him. For the very first time in his life, he was a man who had friends who had cars, who would be happy to lend him their cars.

He asked Deac if he might borrow, probably for the whole day, the VW Polo the boys had hired in London. No problem. The boys would be busy all day. If they wanted to

141

go to the pub they could walk, or take one of the other cars. Deac was not even curious about why Dan wanted a car, or where he was going. He had more important things on his mind. Dan was reminded that, while he was central to what was going on at the Priory, he was also quite outside it. Nobody needed him; nobody even much wanted him, getting in the way and interrupting serious business. The Symposium had taken on guarding his house, feeding his mother and his livestock, and unmasking the Medwell murderer. All he had to do was be properly grateful at the end.

Dan got Harold Dartie's address book, and headed south towards the coast.

There were a dozen towns in Harold Dartie's address book, all on the coast: either seaports like Plymouth or resorts like Bournemouth. Weymouth, where Harold Dartie himself had lived until he went up in the world, was not in the book. Perhaps it had no Indian or Chinese restaurants; perhaps Harold Dartie preferred operating well away from his own doorstep.

The nearest seaside town to Medwell was a place called Yarford, a smallish resort with moderate beaches, one big hotel, a lot of boarding houses, and—in the days when Dan had been infrequently taken there as a child—a smell of fried fish. Three establishments in Yarford figured in Harold Dartie's book. One was called the Viceroy, one the Taj Mahal, one the Taiping Takeaway. Dan thought they were all new since his childhood. The smell of curry would have replaced that of fried fish. The Viceroy was one of those with which he had failed to make contact; its telephone was cut off. The Taiping Takeaway was one of those with which he had had a conversation but a useless one; a high tenor voice had twittered at him like a small bird, like a sedge warbler. The Taj Mahal was run by somebody whose English was pretty good but who denied all knowledge of anybody called Harold Dartie.

142

Dan stopped the Polo just outside Yarford, and rehearsed his approach to these exotics. He was wearing his best blue banker's suit, so that he could be a solicitor or a government health inspector if those seemed useful things to be. He wished he had thought to borrow a briefcase from somebody in the Symposium. He no longer possessed such a thing himself, but his disguise was undoubtedly incomplete without it. The restaurateurs would have to be brave about that. He wished also that he had a photograph of Harold Dartie. The police would have got one from somewhere; they had all kinds of unfair advantages in this sort of situation. Failing a photograph, he should have asked Isabel Robey to do a drawing of Harold Dartie. She had sketched several members of the Symposium, as well as Dan's cottage, and she caught a likeness quite well. Dan felt unprepared and amateurish. He had never had occasion to try anything like this before. But Harold Dartie was so distinctive that Dan thought that, given time, he could successfully describe him even to someone with little English.

He thought he would not be a banker, solicitor, estate agent or government inspector. He thought he would be a journalist, compiling for his paper's readers a list of recommended eating places in south coast resorts. The paper could be the *Milchester Argus*, read weekly, with audible contempt, by Dan's mother. Presumably people from the Milchester area still went to places like Yarford; presumably, when there, they ate meals. It was all pretty credible, Dan thought. He ought to have a pencil and a notebook. The address book could masquerade as a notebook; a small piece of anonymous metal tubing in the car's glove pocket could masquerade as a pencil.

How was Harold Dartie to be brought into the conversation? Ah—it was he who had recommended the restaurant to Dan, who for the purposes of this exercise was arbitrarily called Marcus Bird. Dan wished he knew the Chinese for "recommend" and the Urdu for "iron-grey."

143

There was a lot of traffic on the road. Trucks almost brushed the car, stationary beside the road. The holiday season was still in full swing. Yarford would be crowded. The restaurants and takeaways would presumably be busy at lunchtime, perhaps all day. The time was now, by Dan's mental clock, a little after eleven. They would be busy getting ready for the rush, but not as busy as they would be in an hour or two. It was time to get on.

Probably this was all a waste of time. But he would have been wasting his time at the Priory.

He started the car and drove into the town. Traffic clogged the streets. The sun glared on dusty cars and on the spectacles of middle-aged women in nylon trousers. Two municipal car parks were full; Dan found a third. He walked back into the middle of the town in his little black banker's shoes, sweating in the unaccustomed constriction of collar and tie.

He found the Taiping Takeaway first, a narrow shopfront with a garish yellow sign and a price list in the window. It was already open. Through the plate glass of the window Dan saw two customers, a young couple dressed for the beach. Their sweet-and-sour pork would be gritty with sand. Serving them was a little old man, all smiles, with a black tunic buttoned to the neck. He looked as though he made the sort of noises Dan had heard on the telephone.

The customers collected their lunch, wrapped up in a piece of brown paper. They paid and left.

"Dunno quite what we got," said the young man to his girl, as they came out into the street.

That suggested imperfect communication over the counter. Dan wondered how a man could run a business in England without speaking English.

He went in. The place was small and completely Spartan—nothing but the linoleum on the floor and a metal counter. There was a hatch behind the counter, through which came a smell of cooking and a pleasing chirrup of birdlike voices.

144

The old man got off a stool. He smiled and bowed. He said something, making a noise which was a very fair imitation of a sedge warbler. Perhaps it was intended as "Good morning, sir."

Slowly, slowly, picking short and simple words, Dan delivered his prepared speech. He mentioned Harold Dartie.

"Hada Tati," piped the old man, still smiling but plainly baffled.

Dan thought "recommend" was altogether too long a word to try. He said, "A big, strong man says your food is good. You know him. Tall like this. Grey hair."

He indicated a tall man. He pointed at his own mousy thatch.

He became aware that the twittering from the other side of the hatch had stopped. Two faces appeared in the hatch, an old woman and a younger one. They were listening intently.

Struggling, Dan went on trying to describe Harold Dartie. He imitated his harsh, deep voice. He grimaced to make a face like the grim, thin-lipped face of Harold Dartie.

He thought it was the voice that did it.

The women's twittering burst forth again, directed at the old man, urgent. The old man's smile disappeared.

The old man said, "No no no no no," the first words he had used which came out clearly in English, and about the meaning of which Dan could be certain.

The meaning was that they knew no big strong tall man with grey hair and a harsh voice.

They lied. They were frightened. Dan was going to get nothing out of them at all.

Customers came in, a family party with disgruntled children. The old man turned to them, with a smile which was now forced. Dan had had his chance. He could do no more. He had learned something, but not nearly enough.

He went out to look for the Indian restaurants.

He smelled the Taj Mahal before he saw it, a reek of curry, not unpleasant, coming down a side street. It was a very much grander establishment than the Chinese take-away: broad plate-glass windows each side of a central door, a sign in purple and gold the full width of the façade, huge and heavily decorated menus in the windows. Somebody had been very busy with a fretsaw, creating filigree arches in the Mogul style. Dan had a glimpse of brass lamps and palms in pots. The door stood open; from it belched a warm gust of curry, which made Dan's collar feel even tighter than before. He wanted topee and bush shirt to enter this tropical place.

But he entered it dressed as a banker, or as Marcus Bird, ace gastronomic reporter of the *Milchester Argus.*

He was greeted by a skinny young man with a café-au-lait face and a serious manner. Inside, the decor was oppressively opulent. They had taken a lot of trouble. The result was welcoming, if overwhelming. Nobody was having lunch yet.

Dan announced himself as to the Chinese. In excellent English, the waiter said he would see if Mr Patel was available. Almost immediately he was: a fattish man of about forty with very shiny black hair, wearing a sort of mess jacket with brass buttons. He shook hands with Dan, smiled, and said he was always pleased to welcome the gentlemen of the press. Dan now had no need to speak slowly, or to choose familiar words.

The name Harold Dartie meant no more to Mr Patel than it had on the telephone.

"Perhaps you know him under another name," said Dan.

"How should that be? How should a gentleman give us a false name?"

"Perhaps because he is not really a gentleman," said Dan.

"How should that be?"

The young waiter stopped laying tables and stood listening intently to Dan's description.

"Are you perhaps maybe in truth a policeman?" asked Mr Patel.

Dan was able to look shocked convincingly when he swore that he was not.

Two other skinny waiters came out of the back premises, to listen to Dan's laborious description of Harold Dartie. Mr Patel spoke to them angrily, in a language Dan thought he had never heard. He had no idea which Indian language it was. They replied with equal heat. They were his sons or nephews or cousins, able and more than willing to answer him back. All four of them argued passionately, often glancing at Dan. Their speech did not sound like language. They sounded as much like birds as the Chinese had, but different birds. They were like starlings clicking and hissing at each other, roosting in a dense crowd in a small tree in the evening.

It was obvious to Dan that they knew who he meant, and that they were not going to tell him anything about it.

Mr Patel silenced his relatives at last, and turned back to Dan. "After discussion we conclude that we do not know this gentleman of whom you speak," he said.

Dan thought they thought he was a reporter, but a crime reporter. They did not seem to expect him to taste any food, or look at the menu, or see the kitchen; they had tacitly called his bluff. They were polite about it. They regretted extremely their inability to help him.

They told him where to find the Viceroy, last on the Yarford list; they spread their hands as they directed him. Dan was not sure he correctly read their gesture. They were apologetic, or deprecating, or dismissive; or they were telling him he would have no better luck in the Viceroy.

Dan shook hands all round. Because they were infuriating was no reason not to be polite.

Three minutes later he turned the corner that should take him to the Viceroy. There was no smell of curry. There was no smell of anything. There was no Viceroy. There was an abandoned, roofless building which had had a bad fire. The shops each side had been damaged. One, a butcher, was

147

boarded up and closed for repairs. The other, a news agent, was also boarded up but open, as a sign announced, for business as usual.

"What happened next door?" said Dan to the woman in the news agent's.

"Dunno. They was a parcel o' Wogs. Quiet, you know. Nice enough people. We had the police on us like flies. Somebody put a bomb in there. Them Sikhs, they do say. Always at each other's throats."

"Anybody hurt?"

"Course there was. Breed like rabbits, those blackamoors. Four little kids. All asleep upstairs when it happened. Boom. Then there wasn't no upstairs. Near knocked me out of my chair, an' blew in all our windies. Three o' the kiddies was killed an' one's still what they call critical. We took a collection in the street, all the neighbours, like."

"I'd like to contribute," said Dan, and gave her a pound.

He thought he knew how Harold Dartie had come to be able to afford to buy Medwell Court.

11

THERE HAD BEEN REPORTS, earlier in the year, of tragedies like this. Maybe in other years. Dan remembered talk in the Chestnut Horse in the village.

Harold Dartie had been away from Medwell—was still away, perhaps. Dan thought he knew where he went, and what he did when he got there. "Business," Ted Goldingham had said. Business, indeed.

Dan knew how Harold Dartie had become rich, and he owed the knowledge entirely to the address book. Why had Dartie had the book with him in his hired van, the night he burgled his own house and killed his own security man? Perhaps it was so important to him that he never let it out of his sight. Perhaps it was a sort of talisman, magically necessary for his success. Perhaps he was actually going to use it, later that same night; or perhaps he had already used it, earlier in the night: extracted some more protection money from these helpless little people, or killed some more children with a bomb.

The police could be forgiven for not having got on to any of this. The police had not seen the address book. The address book of itself meant nothing, unless you knew who it belonged to and what kind of man he was. Faced with the book, Harold Dartie would say he had never seen it before. Presumably that was why he had taken the trouble to type out all the addresses. He would not have been particularly worried about losing the book. Nothing linked it to him, except Dan having found it in his briefcase; and he knew by now as well as Dan did that Dan's hands were tied. No doubt he had already compiled the whole thing again, mostly out of the yellow pages. Probably that had been a bore; he would feel no fonder of Dan.

Dan knew why the little old man in the takeaway and the voluble men in the Taj Mahal had told him nothing, had pretended total ignorance, had not been to the police and would not go to them. What happened if you told people about Harold Dartie was that your children were killed.

It had happened to eleven of the restaurants in Harold Dartie's book. *Pour encourager les autres.* Foreign restaurants, ethnic minorities, more or less second-class citizens although a lot of them worked very hard and made good money. Yes—they commonly made more money than the locals because they were clever and well-educated and hard-working. That made them a good target. They were less likely to go to the police, even without the sight of a bombed building in the next street, and less likely to be taken seriously if they did. That also made them a good target. They were people who did indeed, as the woman in the news agent's said, have murderous feuds among themselves; anyway they were thought to do so, which came to the same thing. Sectarian violence in India. Gang warfare among the Chinese, Triads and such, drugs and slavery. A bomb was not so very surprising. It accounted well enough for the pattern which even the police must have spotted—eleven ethnic restaurants destroyed in south coast towns. Why would anyone connect such things with a respectable citizen of Weymouth? Why, God knew, would anybody connect such things with the squire of Medwell Fratrorum?

150

Presumably they posted their money, cash in used notes. Presumably it went to an accommodation address, a box number somewhere, from which it was forwarded or collected. Probably the mechanics were elaborate and just about foolproof, unless some outside factor led you to suspect Harold Dartie: something, for example, like seeing him committing a murder.

This was all still a bit speculative. Dan had researched a sample of only three in a list of something near a hundred. He had time to look at a few more. He thought he wanted to look at some restaurants that no longer had telephones.

There was one place with an unobtainable number in Igton, and one in a little place called Frewmouth. There were other places in both towns to which he had talked on the telephone. Igton was only twenty minutes away, inland and then back to the coast, Frewmouth twenty minutes beyond.

Driving northwest, then southwest, Dan detected a large flaw in his theory. The Viceroy in Yarford had been bombed, either because the Indians who ran it had refused to pay, or because they had gone to the police. So for the other ten places which had presumably been destroyed. Some of those people *must* have been to the police. Harold Dartie *must* have been described, and the accommodation address revealed. The racket *couldn't* have gone on as it had gone on.

The explanation came to Dan. It was so shocking that he had to stop the car. The family who lived over the Viceroy had not been to the police. They had not been subjected to any extortion. They were simply an example. "This is what will happen to you."

Dan looked again at the book. A dozen different towns, eleven silent telephones. The silent telephones—yes—one to a town. No town with two. But one town with no silent telephone. That spoilt the pattern. Dan looked at the road map in the Polo's glove pocket. Two of the towns were really all

151

one town, or one was a suburb of the other. One warning was enough for the restaurateurs of both. Harold Dartie could economise on explosives.

Obviously those bombs had gone off, those fires been lit, those children killed, before the shakedown started in each place. Harold Dartie made no attempt to extort any money until he had destroyed a restaurant, killed a family. After he had done so, he would have had no trouble. Nobody was going to say no to him, and nobody was going to the police. He had made himself absolutely safe, and he had made himself very rich.

Dan felt his mind reeling at such ruthlessness.

Igton was a big, cheerful, down-market resort with a holiday camp, a fun fair, and beaches black with bodies and hideous with transistor radios. All summer, the takeaway trade would be enormous, fish and chips and fried chicken as well as Indian and Chinese. The turnover would be enormous; the profit to Harold Dartie would be enormous, since he had devised his foolproof method of assuring it.

The Star of Madras, a small place in a back street, was being demolished. The building was no longer safe, after the fire they had. Only one person had died, a nephew of the owner's wife, who worked in the kitchen.

Some of the other Indian restaurants in Igton were much bigger and glossier: some grander than the Taj Mahal in Yarford. That made sense. Harold Dartie would sacrifice a comparatively small source of income, and preserve the bigger sources.

Would he feel it necessary, after a year or two, to give them all a reminder? Dan thought it probable. He was a man who took trouble to be safe. It would keep the money coming, as nothing else would.

Could it really all be a one-man operation? A protection racket generally involved a gang of heavies, Dan thought. But it need not, not nowadays, not if you didn't mind who

152

you killed. In the old days, the boss sent in a few hooligans who broke the place up. That was steam-age stuff, and comparatively humane. Modern technology gave you small, powerful bombs detonated by remote control. And he would have been perfectly safe planting the bombs, because nobody knew him. Nobody in the whole town, likely, had ever seen him. The other restaurants saw him after the bang.

He might find it more difficult to plant a bomb if he was doing it not as a warning but as a punishment. Probably he thought that was a problem he would never have to face.

Geographically, too, it looked a one-man affair. Weymouth was almost exactly in the middle of the towns in the address book.

Most of all, Dan thought Harold Dartie was a loner. He wouldn't want to put himself in anybody's power, which you were bound to do if you had help; and he wouldn't want to share the profits.

These thoughts occupied Dan's drive from Igton to Frewmouth, a smaller and altogether more genteel place, which had kept some of its eighteenth-century charm. A bomb in such a place seemed to Dan more shocking, although he knew this was not logical.

The Canton Takeaway—a surprising establishment in such a town—was boarded up and silent. The bang had not been very loud, but it had killed two customers.

Hungry, after driving and legwork and an all too dainty breakfast—hungry in spite of the horrors he had seen and pondered—Dan went to an Indian restaurant in Frewmouth. It was called the New Assam. The food was good and pretty cheap. Business was brisk. A long conversation with the proprietor would have been impossible, unless Dan waited until everyone else had gone away: impossible, and purposeless. The proprietor spoke in his own language to the young waiters, who were probably, again, his relatives. His voice fluted and trilled; he sounded as though he were

153

singing. He was another bird. He was a wren. He looked like a wren, very small and stocky and lively, and like a wren he had a voice of astonishing power from so small a body. Dan hated to think of this congenial, hard-working little man handing over most of his profits to Harold Dartie. But the New Assam was in Harold Dartie's book.

What Dan wanted to do was to take this man, and as many others as the car would hold, back with him to Medwell: and there to face them with Harold Dartie. That would do it. But they'd never come. Dan toyed for a second, crunching a papadum, of kidnapping one or more Indians, just for an evening. Just for Saturday evening. The idea vanished with the last of the papadum.

The trouble was, not one of these people would point a finger at Harold Dartie unless he was already in custody. Even then they might be frightened to do so, in case he had friends. But there was no chance, none, that they would help Dan or anyone else while Harold Dartie was still at large. Therefore Dan must cause Harold Dartie to be arrested, on some quite other grounds. Then some at least of the Indians and Chinese might be emboldened to tell the truth. Probably Harold Dartie had done all kinds of things for which he ought to be arrested, but the only one Dan knew about was the murder of Derek Davis. So the wheel had come full circle; or, to put it more accurately, Dan's project had once again turned itself upside down. At Medwell Priory, and not later than Saturday night, Harold Dartie must be made to convict himself of the Medwell Court murder. Then, and only then, could he be convicted of all the rest.

The Symposium's beloved plan wasn't going to work. What was going to work? Chicken curry and Bombay duck provided no kind of answer.

The drive home was slow and wearisome, the country roads clogged with buses. There was no radio in the car.

Dan amused himself by imitating the voices he had heard,

154

the odd bird voices in the little restaurants. By imitating a sedge warbler, he was doing the voices of the little old man and the two women in the Chinese takeaway; by imitating a flock of starlings in a stunted willow on a summer evening, he was being the Indians in the Taj Mahal; by rendering the loud and various notes of a wren, he was being that nice little man in the New Assam.

Piping, chattering, buzzing, clicking through the open window of the car, he received some odd looks from other drivers. He fell bashfully silent.

He got home in good time to feed his dogs, birds and mother. It was all looked after. He was needed there no more than at the Priory. After a day or two of baffled rage, old Mrs Mallett had adjusted, to an extent which amazed her son, to the busy ministrations of the members of the Symposium. She was being pampered. She liked that. Dan had always tried to pamper her, but it seemed that he was not as good at it as they were. Of course, there were more of them, and they came to it fresh.

There was no sign of Sukie.

Back at the Priory, Dan was given conflicting accounts of the day's achievements. Some said the performance was shaping well, some that it was a shambles.

Marcus Bird—unaware that he was known in south coast towns as a reporter on the *Milchester Argus*—went to the Chestnut Horse to leave a message for Harold Dartie, to invite him to the Symposium's show on Saturday evening. He came back in time for the Nightcap and the singsong. He reported that Harold Dartie had reappeared at the pub; that he had apologised for leaving the previous performance so abruptly, giving as his reason a suddenly remembered commitment to make a telephone call; that he had accepted Marcus Bird's renewed invitation, and promised to stay with it this time.

There had been an obvious, though unstated, possibility that the players would play without a Claudius. Everybody pretended that no such possibility existed, because they were in love with their project. Harold Dartie's apparent reason might have been a prior engagement, or disgust with Dan's non-performance; he might have had all sorts of private reasons. If he was at the Priory, in full view of them all, were Dan's cottage and his mother automatically safe? Probably; there had been no signs of a retinue; but the risk could not possibly be taken. At least three people would have to be at the cottage, even while Harold Dartie was being unmasked. To pick the three was not going to be easy.

During Friday, a sense of urgency—which in Dan's experience did not always have this effect—more or less united the factions into which the Symposium had split. Deac, Chuck, Robin Callender-Smith and Sukie's Aunt Helen showed signs of sinking their differences. Dan understood that the entertainment was beginning to take shape, although he was taking no part in it and was not consulted. They were all very engrossed, including Sukie. The necessity for sentries at Dan's cottage became more than ever irksome; the rehearsal schedule had to be planned round it.

Dan said, "Good night" to Sukie, as the common room emptied.

She said, "Good night," in a flat voice which expressed nothing. Her face expressed nothing.

She went off to bed in the wake of her Aunt Helen, looking like an inscrutable bridesmaid.

Saturday was a day of furious activity, of passionate commitment. Discipline was re-established; everywhere there was evidence of single-mindedness; the inevitable had happened—Sukie's Aunt Helen was in charge. Lesser performing artists, such as Robin Callender-Smith, turned out to be movable objects in the face of that irresistible force.

The three-man guard at Dan's cottage was changed at

156

hourly intervals, in order to give everybody enough re-hearsal time. Old Mrs Mallett watched each changing of the guard with a kind of malevolent amusement. Sometimes she seemed to know exactly what was going on; sometimes not. Dan thought it best to stay away.

Alone of them all, once again, Dan was idle. For the first time in his life he felt lonely. He felt left out. Though he was accepted, he was rejected. He was not rejected any more by Sukie than by the rest of them, but not any less, either. There was no ill will in any of this, except possibly from Sukie; far from it; they were simply too busy to be bothering with him.

Dan had to remind himself that it was his battle they were fighting.

One problem proved intractable, even for Sukie's Aunt Helen. No single member of the Symposium was willing to be absent from the final performance. No member of the di-recting staff was, either. It was hard to blame them. Though only the most decorative supporting role could be found in the drama for, for example, Geoffrey Farland, the Exeter es-tate agent, and his antique flutes, he argued that participa-tion in the performance was part of what he had paid his fee for. This argument, though crude, was found unanswerable; Marcus Bird was not inclined to make refunds.

The solution pleased everybody, except old Mrs Mallett: the Priory caretakers, George and Ivy Plummer, were taken down to the cottage in the early evening. George was a burly fellow, Ivy burlier. It was a brave man who would take on the pair of them. They would be relieved in the late evening, by which time the murderer would have been unmasked.

Nobody was in any doubt of this, except Dan, whose opinion carried no weight.

As on the previous Saturday, they had an early supper; as then, there was a neurotic and inward-looking atmosphere.

157

Dan was oppressed by it. He was oppressed by his own certainty that none of this was going to work; that he had somehow, before lunch the following day, to do something which he had no glimmering of an idea how to do. He was oppressed by Sukie's inscrutable stare, and by the way she kept away from him.

The structure of the evening was to be much as before, with the differences only that the order of events was exactly planned in advance, and that Dan was not involved to spoil everything. Margot Dean's lights had been left in position over the arch, and the upright piano was in the same place. All the performers not on stage at any given moment would be in the audience. There was an extra reason for this, on top of the non-stop fluidity it promised: the whole Symposium would be witness of the unmasking.

Harold Dartie arrived. Already performance was necessary, from Marcus Bird and his staff as well as from the performers: they had to pretend to welcome him, to like and respect him, to look forward to his opinion and to his future support.

He was placed not near the end of the semicircle of chairs, but in the middle. This was so that everybody would be able to see the working of his face when he found himself exposed, and so that he could be instantly surrounded if he tried to make a break for it.

Dan saw that there was another outsider, inconspicuous at the end of the hall. Dan wondered if Marcus Bird, or one of the others, had brought along a policeman. It was supremely pointless. It would have been a good idea, if only the *Hamlet* plan had a chance of working.

Harold Dartie saw Dan. His stare was as inscrutable as Sukie's. He could wait. He only had eighteen hours to wait, and then the cobweb would be empty of all except fly and spider. Dan thought he himself was the reason Harold Dartie had done something so eccentric as to accept Marcus Bird's invitation. He was making sure that Dan was still

158

about, and would be available for interrogation the following day.

Harold Dartie seemed a creature of a different species from the Symposium members who surrounded him. He wore a decent dark suit, much like, though much larger than, the one Dan had worn to the coast. The others were all more or less fantastically garbed. Sukie's Aunt Helen's cheeks were once again rouged like a doll's. Sukie had a spare leotard, which did no less for her figure than the one Harold Dartie had ruined. Dan saw Harold Dartie looking hard at her too. He must have assumed by now that she had not identified him, the night he was about to break all her fingers. But he could not have been quite sure.

All the Symposium had been more or less touched by the sun, after a fortnight of fine weather, much of which they had spent out of doors. Harold Dartie's face was still as white as a pine plank, and looked as though it was carved out of pine.

Dan felt a wave of affection and gratitude for all his new friends. They *were* a different species from Harold Dartie. It was just a pity they were taking so much trouble for nothing.

Silence began to fall. Marcus Bird rang the hand bell which was used, in term time, for the little girls' fire drill. Presently Jeremy Chalice came with a certain false jauntiness through the door of the classroom behind the stage— the one through which Dan had made his ignominious escape the week before. Jeremy sat with his guitar on the steps at the end of the hall.

> We have a story to unfold
> To make a statue's blood run cold . . .

It was another modern folk song, composed during the previous couple of days; the tune was more or less the same as that of all Jeremy's songs; his voice was very clear and his diction excellent.

159

Harold Dartie looked as though he had no idea what Jeremy Chalice was on about.

Offstage voices swelled the chorus:

> He'll go pale and he'll go red,
> Like the blood of the man that's dead—
> He'll go red and he'll go pale,
> And he'll spend fifty years in jail.

The voices were those of Deac and Chuck, who now, in ringmaster's top hat and clown's nose, burst out of the classroom into the glare of the lights. They introduced the Imaginary Circus. Changing hats and noses, they mimed a lion-taming act. The lion (Deac) mauled the lion-tamer (Chuck). The lion was then shot by a lion-shooter (Chuck). In case the message of retribution was not sufficiently clear, it was explained by a further verse of Jeremy Chalice's song.

Dan thought the young Americans were really very good; Deac, snarling and lashing an imaginary tail, was a lion which gradually realised that it had a moral advantage, that its tamer was frightened; Chuck, holding a kitchen chair and cracking an imaginary whip, visibly lost his nerve. But it was a little long. By the time Chuck pointed his forefinger at Deac and said "Bang," Dan's chair was beginning to feel hard.

It became clear, as act followed act, that it was all going to take far, far longer than anyone had expected. Now that they were actually doing it under the lights, a certain expansiveness, even self-indulgence, entered the performances of the artists. George and Ivy Plummer would be sitting in the kitchen of Dan's cottage pretty well until midnight. By then Dan's chair—presumably Harold Dartie's too—would be feeling very hard indeed.

A kind of Everyman, represented by Maxwell Piper, the Reading dentist, pressed his nose against an imaginary plate-glass window. Sukie, lovely in her leotard, mimed Envy.

160

An ill-defined crime was committed. Maxwell Piper, on its proceeds, bought silver from one of Robin Callender-Smith's life-size puppets. He crooned over it. Sukie mimed Lust. She was not erotic about it, because what she was lusting for was more silver, or more money.

The progress of events was explained either by the young Americans, as ringmaster and clown, or by further verses from Jeremy Chalice. They had all written far too much material for themselves.

The imaginary silver was valued and insured. Sukie's Aunt Helen performed a dance expressive of the great value of the silver. Had Dan not felt so far from laughing he would have felt close to laughing. At the same time he was impressed; he would have said that it was impossible to express a high insurance valuation on a piece of silver by means of dancing about with rouge on your cheeks: but Sukie's Aunt Helen did it. But she went on doing it rather long.

The treasure was transferred from one place to another. A guard was set on it. Geoffrey Farland's antique flageolet played a nocturne, signifying the depths of night.

Sukie mimed Greed.

The murder. The witness to the murder, the role of Dan being played by Isabel Robey.

The guard's grieving family. The bafflement of the police. The threat to Dan's cottage, and the guard placed on it. And on, and on, and on. The individual contributions still seemed to Dan excellent, especially Sukie's, but as a whole the performance dragged.

Harold Dartie watched impassively. He clapped when the others clapped, and made at least a pretence of laughing when the others laughed. Marcus Bird kept stealing glances at him. Everybody kept stealing glances at him. He could not have been unaware of those glances. He could not have been unaware of what the whole performance was about. He did not do what he was supposed to do. His face did not go red; it did not go pale, because it was pale already.

161

Finale. The whole Symposium stood in a circle round Harold Dartie. Marcus Bird had slipped away from his seat, so that Harold Dartie sat all alone. Every forefinger raised accusingly, pointed at Harold Dartie. The whole Symposium sang the chorus from Jeremy Chalice's song.

Harold Dartie smiled a thin-lipped smile. At the end of the song he clapped, all alone, the single member of the audience except for Dan. Dan, without in the least understanding why, clapped also.

And that was it.

12

HAROLD DARTIE STOPPED CLAPPING; so did Dan. Dan realised that the self-effacing man at the back of the hall, whom
he took to be a policeman, was clapping also; he too stopped.

There was a moment of complete silence. A cloud of despair hung almost visibly over the Symposium; an aura of
sublime confidence radiated from Harold Dartie.

Into the silence, from the depths of the Priory Woods,
came the hoot of an owl.

Birds.

Dan supposed that the owl made him think about birds,
and birds gave him the idea.

Dan cleared his throat nervously, and called out, "Marcus,
I think it's time our other guests met Mr Dartie."

Surprised, Marcus Bird glanced at the man at the back of
the hall. The man shrugged. He had been wasting his time.
He looked as though he had known all along exactly how it
would be.

"No, I mean our *other* visitors," said Dan. "The Indians
and Chinese."

They all looked at him in absolute bafflement. There
seemed to be, for a second, a kind of red glare behind Harold
Dartie's eyes.

Dan pulled the address book out of his pocket.

"That nice Mr Patel," he said, "from the Taj Mahal in Yarford. That nice old Chinaman from the Taiping Takeaway. Of course the people from the Viceroy couldn't come. The child who wasn't killed is still on the critical list."

"Critical list," repeated Marcus Bird blankly.

"But, Dan," said Sukie's Aunt Helen, "there isn't anybody here like that."

"No, I don't think there is," said Harold Dartie unexpectedly, in his deep harsh voice.

At that moment, Dan thought, Harold Dartie saw his address book in Dan's hand. The red glare came and went. His hand twitched. But the one thing he would never, ever, do was claim the book for his own.

It was probably impossible to bluff him. Dan thought he had better go on trying.

"That's what I was doing on Wednesday," said Dan. "That's what I wanted the car for. Tour of coastal resorts. Most revealing. Very frightened people, but I told them they'd be safe with us. They wouldn't have dared identify him, but now they will."

"What nonsense is this?" said Harold Dartie to Marcus Bird. He was evidently angry but his anger was under control. Marcus Bird recoiled. He was evidently frightened and his fright was only barely under control.

The bluff was by no means working yet.

"I'll get them in," said Dan.

He went towards the door of the furthest classroom, which had not been used in the performance.

As he went he called out, loud enough to be heard at the other end of Medwell, "Mr Patel! Will you and the others come this way? I think your troubles are over!"

He glanced back as he reached the door. Harold Dartie had not moved. He did not believe that anything would have given those little Orientals courage to come and expose him. He was quite right. In five seconds Dan's bluff would be

164

called, and all would be as it was, until after lunch next day.

Dan opened the door of the classroom.

Using a wheedling, cajoling tone, softer but loud enough for them all to hear, he said, "Mr Patel! You promised! No harm can come to you now. And you, my friend, and you."

He glanced back again. The Symposium were all looking at him blankly as when he had dried up the week before. Harold Dartie gave a brief bark of humourless laughter.

Birds. He would fill the room with birds.

He went into the classroom, leaving the door open. He went only a little way in, so that his voice could still be heard in the hall.

He called out, "You're quite safe here, Mr Patel."

He answered himself with the remembered cackle and jabber of a starling in a crowd of starlings in a small tree in the evening.

"Good!" he called out. "And you, my friend."

He answered himself in the piping and rattling of the old Chinese's sedge warbler imitation.

"Come along, then, all of you—we don't want to keep Mr Dartie waiting."

He answered himself with the voice of a baritone wren, the voice of the wren-like man in the New Assam in Frewmouth.

He alternated starling, sedge warbler and wren. He put in a bit of the rapid, melodious stammer of a swallow, which might sound like a kind of Chinese, and the sour whine of a greenfinch, which might be the noise made by an Indian frightened of exposing his extortioner; he did a yellowhammer, thinking of it as a scribbling lark.

There was a female scream from the hall, male shouts, what sounded like an order, a great tumbling of folding chairs.

Dan ran out of the classroom. The place was a shambles. Several people were on the floor, or struggling up from it. The nondescript man by the outside door was on his hands

165

and knees, apparently hurt. There was banging and shouting in the porch outside; then silence.

A uniformed policeman came in, distinctly tousled. He helped his superior officer to his feet.

"By gum, that bloke's strong," he said. "Took four of us. Anyway the cuffs are on him now." To Dan he said, "Amazing effect it had, didn't it, the prospect of meeting those people? Seemed he just couldn't stomach it. We'll take statements from them now, since we've got them here. I daresay we'll understand why he didn't want to meet them. They all speak a bit of English, I suppose? It's funny how when they're jabbering away they sound like a flock of birds."

The injuries to the Symposium were slight. Harold Dartie had simply burst through the ring which surrounded him, shaking off restraining hands, tearing one dress and breaking one pair of spectacles. The plain-clothes officer by the door had tried to stop him, and been punched in the solar plexus. It was fortunate that there were four—and not less than four—uniformed constables outside.

Dan understood that, if he could contrive not to be seen by his victims, Harold Dartie would still have been safe. It was worth risking the consequences of an assault on the police, not to be identified by the likes of Mr Patel.

It was annoying for the police that they had to take Harold Dartie all the way to Yarford, Igton, Frewmouth, and so forth, to be identified by people in his address book; they had thought much trouble would be saved by Dan's friends being in the classroom.

Dan said he had found the address book in the car park of the Chestnut Horse. He could not return it to its owner, because there was no way of knowing who the owner was. He offered it to a policeman, who looked at him a little oddly, but took it.

There was, and remained, a crowd round Dan, touching him and calling to him and bombarding him with questions.

166

He suddenly wanted to be out of the crowd. He wanted to be out of doors. He wanted to hear the owl again, the mysterious questioning note from the depths of the Priory Woods.

Having difficulty making himself heard, he said, "I'll go and tell George and Ivy Plummer they can pack up and go to bed."

"I'll come with you," said a voice he had hardly heard for days.

"What were those birds?" said Sukie, as they strolled across the dark lawn. "I don't care what birds they were. What I want to know is, what's wrong with me?"

"Nothing."

"There has to be something terribly wrong with me. I never used to think there was. Other guys don't seem to think there is. Do I have a birthmark I can't see? Do I have bad breath?"

"No."

"Chuck and Deac said everybody in that pub said no girl was safe from you. Why am I so goddam safe from you?"

"Oh," said Dan, so astonished that he stopped dead. "Is that what's been annoying you?"

"Well, certainly puzzling me. Obviously, if you had that kind of a reputation, and there I was around you all of every day, there had to be something horribly wrong with me. That's the only way to explain why I didn't have to worry about you."

"You do have to worry about me," said Dan. "You're not safe at all. You're in the most hideous danger."

He kissed her, for quite a long time, because it was the first.

"You're right," she said into his cheek. "I never was in worse danger."

"I think George and Ivy Plummer can wait a bit," said Dan.

"I think they can."

167